PRAISE FOR
JOE R. LANSDALE

Award-winning author of *The Drive-In*,
The Magic Wagon, and *Nightrunners*

"Razor brilliant. Redline passion. Lansdale is a great writer."
—RICHARD CHRISTIAN MATHESON, author of *Scars*

"Vivid imagination!"   —*Fangoria*

"Reading Lansdale's work is like watching a Texas thunderhead rolling across the plains: darkly beautiful as it builds, but God help you when the storm breaks!"
—CRAIG SPECTOR, coauthor of *The Scream*

"Lansdale has a talent for unnerving the reader by showing us the monster in ourselves."
—*Fort Lauderdale News/Sun-Sentinel*

"[His] prose leaps off the page!"
—*Mystery Scene*

Bestsellers Guaranteed

Joe R. Lansdale

ACE BOOKS, NEW YORK

The novella ''The Events Concerning a Nude Fold-Out Found in a Harlequin Romance'' first appeared in the collection *Dark at Heart* published by Dark Harvest Press in 1992. All other stories in this collection appeared in the anthology *Stories by Mama Lansdale's Youngest Boy* from Pulphouse Publishing in 1991.

BESTSELLERS GUARANTEED

An Ace Book / published by arrangement with
the author

PRINTING HISTORY
Ace edition / May 1993

ISBN: 0-441-05502-8

Ace Books are published by The Berkley Publishing Group,
200 Madison Avenue, New York, New York 10016.
The name ''ACE'' and the ''A'' logo
are trademarks belonging to Charter Communications, Inc.

PRINTED IN THE UNITED STATES OF AMERICA

10   9   8   7   6   5   4   3   2   1

Contents

Introduction

This is my second short story collection, sort of. Actually, this collection first appeared in a slightly different version under the title *Stories by Mama Lansdale's Youngest Boy* from Pulphouse Publishing. It is being presented here in a somewhat revised version, with a new novella added. The novella, "The Events Concerning a Nude Fold-Out Found in a Harlequin Romance," first appeared in *Dark at Heart*, an anthology edited by my wife, Karen, and myself.

With the exception of "The Job" and the aforementioned novella, most of the stories represented here are earlier stories.

I believe the stories in my first collection, *By Bizarre Hands*, better characterize the writer I am today, though a number of those were written alongside these chronologically.

But I hasten to add I am in no way trying to pawn off crap for a quick buck by putting together this collection. I like these stories. They show their influences a bit more readily than my current work, but they're stories of mine I've reread and enjoyed, and many of them represent turning points in my career, or they're stories that seem to have been popular with readers—to the point of being photocopied repeatedly and passed around—but for some reason or another were never reprinted, or were reprinted in out-of-the-way publications. I'm glad to have this opportunity to make them more readily available. I've touched them up a bit, but have made no major rewrites. I think the stories should appear as they first came out, with the exception of obvious spelling errors, typos, or a sentence that just plain doesn't do what it was intended to do, or is so tin-eared it distracts from the story.

Early in my career, as with most writers, I found it very difficult to get my work published, and because of this, it was less daunting to spend a few days to a week on a short story instead of months on a novel that might be rejected. A short investment of time and the fact that I could have a dozen or more short stories working for me instead of one novel was very appealing. There was also the fact that I needed money, and though I wasn't making any killing with the sale of my short stories, fifty dollars here, a hundred dollars there was preferable to all the rejects I got on such novels as *Act of Love, Dead in the West,* and *The Nightrunners.* (Novels, I might add, that have gone on to be reprinted and look to have more of a life than I ever suspected.) There was also this: I prefer writing short stories most of the time. I wouldn't want to give up novels, screenplays, comic scripts, stage plays, non-fiction, etc., but if it came down to choosing which I prefer, I'd have to say short stories. In fact, I like them more than ever because I feel I've learned better how to write them, how to do more than just put a twist at the end.

But the fact remains, novels work harder for a writer and are more likely to bring attention to that writer's short stories than his or her short stories bringing attention to the novels.

Though I've been heavily influenced by a lot of writers, the hard-boiled detective and suspense writers especially, the writers who influenced most of the stories in this book are the American greats of the horror/fantasy field. Ray Bradbury, Richard Matheson, William F. Nolan, Robert Bloch, Fred Brown, and Charles Beaumont, also lesser known writers like Robert Arthur and Gerald Kersh. There is also a touch of the English—E. F. Benson, M. R. James, and Arthur Conan Doyle—though admittedly their influence is more muted, damn near subliminal, you might say, but they're here nonetheless. I also like to think the first inklings of my current and truer writing voice are here as well. A voice much inspired by the tall tales and voices of East Texans.

I'll pause now for a quick note of biography.

My interest in writing has been with me for as long as I can remember. My first work dates from when I was nine years old. A poem about my dog, if memory serves me. I grew up loving words and what they could do. I liked film too, and it has obviously influenced my work, but it was always the words that counted, and as I grow older, they count even more.

I read everything from fairy tales to books on lost civilizations to horror to mystery to adventure to the classics to comics, especially "Batman" and "Detective Comics." I had no idea that one type of fiction or non-fiction was supposedly better for me than another. I think this is one of the most fortuitous things about my career. Ignorance.

I read what appealed to me, not what was supposed to be good for me. That being the case, it was only natural that I would gradually mix genres, and eventually run them through the mental strainer of my East Texas experience to arrive at the sort of stories that appeared in *By Bizarre Hands*, and the sort of stories I write now. These are among the best of the stories I wrote on the way to that destination. I like to think it was a pretty good trip, and that I'll be starting a new trip soon, branching out from what I do now, going yet another mile and finding new passions, new stories.

I hope these stories amuse you, entertain on one level or another, for that is their prime directive. I wrote them to entertain myself, hoping others out there would like what entertained me.

A few of these stories have recent publication dates, but the bulk of them were written when I was beginning as a writer and was having a hard time placing them. Therefore, the copyright page will not necessarily reflect when they were created, and I've purposely avoided printing them in the order of their creation or first appearance because I thought it better to arrange them for impact, not autobiography.

Probably a stupid idea, since most of the time I spot-read collections, starting with titles that appeal, or first sentences that leap out and grab me and suck me in, and I wouldn't be surprised if it's the same with most readers.

Lastly, I'd like to say that the original title for this collection, *Stories by Mama Lansdale's Youngest Boy*, was for a reason, other than the obviously humorous one. My mother was the first to encourage my love of the written word. She made sure I had a library card, and when we could afford them, books. Her dedication to supplying me with books and encouraging me to become a writer— though like most moms she would have preferred I had what she so often referred to as "Something to fall back on"—contributed to making my life a happy and exciting one. In fact, writing has opened so many doors for me I occasionally have to sit and wonder if it's all a dream. I've been able to move out of the backbreaking work I used to do into something more substantial, and if I can't honestly say it's easier, I can say it's more satisfying. It sure beats cleaning toilets and digging ditches.

It has afforded me the opportunity to meet a lot of interesting and fascinating people, as well as a few assholes, but hey, that's all right too. It's allowed me to travel to places I thought I might never see, and best of all, I think it's helped me understand myself better, comment on things that concern me, entertain myself, and now that I'm making a few bucks, that doesn't hurt my feelings either.

So, even though the stories contained herein are probably not the sort to her liking, I dedicate this book to my mother, Reta Lansdale Cronn, with love.

Enough of this.

The stories.

The White Rabbit

This is the oldest story in the collection, and though I said in the intro that I haven't arranged these stories in order of appearance, by coincidence, this one is appearing first.

I wrote it for an anthology titled GHOUL! that Bill Pronzini, a very good writer of mysteries, was editing. I wrote two others previous to it for his anthologies MUMMY! and CREATURE! but this one was the first of the three I really liked, and the first story that made me feel I might actually have something inside me that was unique. I'm not sure why that was, or even if I'm accurate on the matter, and certainly the story shows some age now, but the writing of it was a revelation for me, probably because it was the first story of mine that seemed to write itself, and it mixed genres thoughtlessly. If I make a conscious effort to mix them, I can't. It has to flow, and this was the first story of mine that flowed.

Inspiration for it is obvious. ALICE IN WONDERLAND. I had been rereading it, and that night I ate popcorn, and . . . well, the influence of popcorn will be explained in another introduction. Enjoy "The White Rabbit."

For Bill Pronzini

One moment he had been comfortably reading, for the umpteenth time, ALICE IN WONDERLAND, and the next moment it was too stuffy and hot to concentrate. The words seemed to melt and re-form before his eyes, and he found himself slipping in and out of sleep like nervous fingers first filling, then withdrawing from a glove.

Sleepy, but being a man of strict routine, he put the book aside, left his tacky hotel room—the Egyptians here in Cairo thought it a fine place—and took to the streets in the dead of night.

It was warm out, but more comfortable than his room. Out here was like sitting in an oven with the door open, as opposed to the room, which was more like sitting in an oven with the door closed.

Yet, in spite of the stickiness of the night, the air had an intoxicating feel. The streets, buildings, all that should be familiar, had an oddly haunting, slightly alien look about it, as if they had been replaced with facsimiles of the originals. Even his footsteps on the cobblestones seemed strangely distant. Odder yet, there was neither street urchin nor curled sleeping beggar in sight. More often than not, they lay against the walls of buildings, or in the doorways, like abandoned curs. But tonight . . . no one.

Wally Carpenter knew that to walk these streets late at night was to invite trouble, but he was not a fearful man. And besides, he carried in his coat pocket a fully loaded, .38 snub-nose revolver, with which he was rather proficient.

So it was with caution, but no particular dread, that Carpenter stalked Cairo's dark streets and pondered upon the seeming emptiness and uncharacteristic silence of the city. He wandered in a nearly aimless fashion, feeling for all the world as though he had been hijacked by space creatures and set down in a replica of the city he knew and loved; and presently his footsteps brought him to that area of Cairo known as the City of the Dead.

The place was quite a marvel. An entire city—houses, streets, and walls—devoted to the spirits of the recent and the long departed. It was said that there were men in Cairo who had the ability to speak with these dead and for a fee they would summon the spirits of loved ones and communicate questions to them, and return their answers.

It was a mystical place, a place shrouded in legend, and not a good spot for a person, especially a non-Egyptian, to wander late at night. Robbers and lepers were said to frequent the city, and it was also said to be the home of demons and ghouls.

Carpenter was well aware of this, but it did not concern him. His revolver could dispatch robbers, and as for ghouls and such, he did not believe in them; they were the stuff of opium dreams and fevered imaginations, nothing more.

Once Carpenter had been a student, a promising one at that. He had majored in anthropology and archaeology, and those fields of endeavor had brought him to Egypt, land of antiquity, land of dreams.

But once he had dug in its sands and prowled its tombs, he lost interest in the physical work of the profession, decided he was more suited to the academic side of the subject. He determined to write a book, to deal in paper and ink instead of dirt and sweat.

That decision made, he often walked the streets at night, made his mental notes and later consigned them to paper, saved them up against the day he would write his book on the wonders and marvels of Egypt. In the meanwhile, he read his archaeology, mythology and anthropology texts, and in his spare time, for pure amusement, he read and reread Lewis Carroll's ALICE IN WONDERLAND, as well as its sequel, THROUGH THE LOOKING GLASS. Carroll's was the only fiction he truly cared for. It relaxed him, made him smile, and each time he read the books, he found something new and fascinating within. In fact, Alice and her adventures were still in his head as he reached the City of the Dead and made his way within.

Walking among the ruins he could smell the rank ripeness of decay, as well as the mixed and confusing odors of Cairo proper. But the smells seemed oddly received by his senses, as if they were being filtered to him from another dimension. It was quiet and peaceful here, like stepping off the earth and standing on the face of the moon.

But even as he dwelled on the solitude, there came a scuttling sound to his right. Carpenter turned quickly, saw a figure move from one clump of shadows to another, flitter once in the moonlight, then disappear totally into darkness.

Carpenter almost pulled the revolver from his coat pocket. It could be a robber, but most likely it was a beggar or a leper who had taken refuge here, much in the same way tramps back in the states slept in graveyards to avoid being disturbed. If the latter were the case, then there would be little to fear. If it was a robber, then he had his revolver.

He strained his eyes into the darkness, but saw nothing. Presently he began to walk again. He had not gone ten feet when he heard the scuttling again, and this time, as he turned, he saw the author of the noise.

Out of the shadows hopped a huge white rabbit wearing a checkered waistcoat and vest. The rabbit stopped, gave Carpenter a disinterested glance, then plucked a pocket watch from his waistcoat pocket.

"Oh my goodness, goodness," the rabbit said in remarkably plain English. "I shall be late. Yes, yes, yes, so very late."

Turning, and with a succession of rapid hops, the rabbit disappeared back into the shadows.

Carpenter shook his head, blinked a few times. Yes, it *was* an intoxicating night, all right, but this was ridiculous. Six-foot rabbits in Cairo? In the City of the Dead? Shades of *Harvey*. He must be dreaming.

Suddenly there came the sound of melodious humming. Carpenter recognized the tune. It was the song that George

Armstrong Custer had adopted as his personal theme. What was it called? "Garry Owen"? Yes, something like that.

The humming faded off into the night. Pulling his revolver, Carpenter strolled briskly into the shadows, determined to find out why there was a rabbit-suited joker hopping about in the City of the Dead humming "Garry Owen."

He could hear the humming again. It seemed to come from far away. Carpenter continued forward and the velvet night closed tight around him. He came to an obstruction and, lighting a match, he saw that it was an adobe wall. Just to his left was a large, round opening. It appeared to have been knocked into the clay. Beyond the wall, he could hear the faint humming of "Garry Owen."

Stooping, match in one hand, revolver in the other, Carpenter stepped through the opening.

Once on the other side he stopped and looked about. No rabbit.

The match went out. But there was no need for it now. It was suddenly very bright, much brighter than before. Above him the moon shone like an aluminum skillet and the stars looked down like millions of bright, animal eyes peering out of the darkness of a wood.

"Odd, quite odd," Carpenter said aloud. He thought: I must be sitting at home in my chair fast asleep, having fallen off reading ALICE IN WONDERLAND, and now I'm dreaming all this. "Curiouser and curiouser!" he said in self-mockery.

"Oh my, my," the rabbit's voice came again, and the big bunny seemed to come out of nowhere and hop by. The rabbit's white, fluffy tail bobbed before Carpenter like a bounding ball.

"Hey you, wait a minute!" Carpenter yelled.

The rabbit stopped, turned to look over its shoulder. "Goodness, goodness, what is it? Make it quick. I'm so late, so very late."

Carpenter, feeling a bit stupid about the revolver, returned it to his coat pocket. It hardly seemed sporting to shoot a giant bunny. He walked quickly over to the rabbit, shook his head and said, "It's not a suit."

"What?" the rabbit said.

"I *am* dreaming, must be. Giant rabbits, indeed."

The rabbit turned completely about and faced Carpenter, wriggled its ample pink nose, flashed its pink eyes. "Let's not dismiss rabbits, shall we?" The rabbit produced a small fan and patted it into the palm of his other paw (hand?).

"This is ridiculous," Carpenter said. "I can't wake up."

"Is it now? Can't you now?" the rabbit said sharply.

"A crazy dream. I feel as if I've fallen down a rabbit hole."

"Quite possible, quite possible," the rabbit said. "There are holes all over the universe, you know. Whitechapel, England; Fall River, Massachusetts. All over. They pop up all manner of places, yes they do."

"This is all rather inconceivable," Carpenter said.

"Is it now?" the rabbit said as if truly surprised. " 'What song the Sirens sang, or what name Achilles assumed when he hid himself among women, though puzzling questions, are not beyond all conjecture.' " The rabbit bowed. "Sir Thomas Browne."

"Yes . . . Very nice. Where am I? Can this be the City of the Dead? A dream?"

" 'There are countless roads on all sides of the grave,' " the rabbit said. "Cicero."

"Now what kind of answer is that?" Carpenter said.

The rabbit produced the pocket watch from his waistcoat pocket again. "Oh filly fuddles. I am wasting time. Come, come if you must, but hurry."

For a moment Carpenter stood dumbfounded, then finally followed the rabbit, who was making rather remarkable time with his hops. It was quite a merry chase, and presently

Carpenter came upon the rabbit again. The big bunny was sitting on a stone bench next to a metal light pole reading a newspaper. A piece of paper taped to the light pole fluttered in the wind, and a handful of large bugs swarmed in the overhead glow. At the rabbit's feet a horde of passionflowers grew, along with purple-flowered belladonna plants.

"I thought you were late," Carpenter said.

"Late?" the rabbit asked.

"I thought . . . Oh, never mind. I can't believe I'm talking to a rabbit."

"And why not?" the rabbit said, dropping the paper to his lap. His nose wriggled in an impatient sort of way.

"Well, you couldn't be real."

The rabbit crossed his left leg over his right knee and swung his foot nervously. The newspaper fluttered to the ground. "My goodness, but you are silly. So hard to convince, so hard." The rabbit raised his voice, pointed at Carpenter. "Believe it hard enough and it is true."

"But six-foot rabbits! Rabbits are small, insignificant creatures."

The rabbit stood to its full height. "I'll have you know we are quite revered, quite. Why, the very god of Egypt's antiquity was rabbit-headed. Yes he was, he was."

Carpenter considered. Yes, in fact, Osiris, God of the Dead, was often depicted as a rabbit-headed god. In that guise he was usually known as Wenenu.

"But where am I?" Carpenter asked the rabbit.

"You are here, that is where you are," the rabbit said. "My goodness, such silly questions."

Carpenter scratched his head. "You said there were holes all over the universe. Could I have fallen into one of those?"

"Oh, quite possible, quite. There are holes all over the place. Whitechapel, for instance." And with that, the rabbit went into a little dance, chanted a rhyme.

"Jack the Ripper's dead.
And lying on his bed.
He cut his throat
With sunlight soap.
Jack the Ripper's dead."

The rabbit paused and said, "Fall River also." The dance began again, a sort of highlander jig.

"Lizzie Borden took an ax
And gave her mother forty whacks.
When she saw what she had done
She gave her father forty-one!"

The rabbit stopped dancing, leaned forward, showed Carpenter its two front teeth, both as bright and thick as huge sugar cubes. "Or did she?" the rabbit whispered.

"Very nice," Carpenter said, getting into the spirit of things. "A very fine dance."

"Oh," the rabbit said with obvious pleasure, "you really think so?"

"I do."

The rabbit made an effort to appear modest. "Well, I do have a certain knack for it, you know?"

"I can see that."

"Can you now? Good, good." Then, almost confessionally, "There are a lot of rabbits, you know. Pop up anywhere and everywhere." The rabbit gave Carpenter a sly wink. "Take a look at that paper on the light pole there, sir. Very enlightening, very."

Carpenter turned to the light pole, to the paper fluttering there. The wind had picked up and was making quite a production of it. It nearly managed to rip the taped paper from the pole. Carpenter reached his glasses from his pocket, put them on for a look-see.

The wind died as suddenly as it had come up, and Carpenter bent forward to read the little paper. It appeared to be a page precisely torn from a medical journal. A stamp at the top of it alerted him that the page had once been included in a book contained in the United States Army Medical Library in Washington.

Reading, Carpenter found the page concerned the matter of one Mary Toft, a woman who, in 1726, claimed to have given birth to twelve baby rabbits. Although this incident was never proven to be true, neither was it disproved.

"Astounding," Carpenter said, putting his glasses away, turning toward the rabbit. But the rabbit was gone. Carpenter could see him hopping in the distance, disappearing once again into the darkness.

The wind came again, and it stirred the paper that had fallen from the rabbit's lap, wrapped it around Carpenter's ankles. He dislodged it, and was about to toss it aside when an article outlined in red caught his eye. He did not bother with his glasses this time, but instead pushed it close to his face.

It was a short little article dealing with the brutal deaths of several black New York cabbies. They had been killed in their cabs and their hearts cut out. The article said there were no clues.

Carpenter shivered, tossed the paper away, looked about. Things had changed. He had not been aware of the moment of change, but this no longer appeared to be the City of the Dead. In the distance, silhouetted by the moon, were shapes that reminded him of the place, but here, close up, all was very different. The bench and light post, for instance. Where in the world had they come from?

There was something else. The feel. Not something you could put your finger on, but something you could sense in much the same way you could sense the changing of climate. Yes, something was very different.

For lack of better things to do, Carpenter strolled toward where he had last seen the rabbit. As he walked, he noticed on his left a great vista of bombed-out houses and buildings. It looked much as he thought London must have looked after the Germans tried to abolish the city with their blitzkrieg.

To his right there was a huge cart piled high with something encased in shadows. A horse was hitched to the cart and it held its head dipped toward the stones. Smoke rose in the distance beyond the cart, and somewhere, faintly, came a voice calling, "Bring out your dead."

Carpenter walked briskly, the visions on either side of him melting away like fading motion picture images.

"Do you think perhaps it's done with mirrors?" the rabbit asked, stepping from the darkness.

"I . . . I thought you were ahead of me. How did you do that?"

"I put this foot in front of this one," the rabbit said. "Quite simple, really."

"I mean how . . . never mind."

The rabbit produced the pocket watch again. "Oh, I must hurry."

"I thought you weren't late."

"You did? Why would you get such an idea? I am late, you know. Murdering time, murdering time."

"Late for the tea party?"

"Tea party? I don't drink tea. What tea party is that?"

"Never mind."

The rabbit looked at his watch again. "Goodness yes. I must hop." And away went the rabbit, singing the Jack the Ripper chant again, only this time substituting other words.

> "Jack the Rabbit's dead
> And living in your head
> Cut his throat on moonlight rope,
> Jack the Rabbit's dead."

Carpenter found himself practically running to keep up with the rabbit. Soon he came to a long, seven-foot-high rock wall. Like the first wall, there was a large hole in it. The hole led into total blackness. Carpenter's last sight of the rabbit had been as the creature, ducking somewhat to fit, hopped through the hole and disappeared.

"When in Rome or whatever," Carpenter said, "do as the Romans or the whatevers." With that he stepped through the hole into the dark . . . felt as if he were drifting. There was a loud ticking sound, *tick, tick, tick,* like some sort of giant clock. Then came a swooshing, like sand drifting down into the bottom of an hourglass, followed by complete and total silence.

I *must* be at home asleep in my chair, he thought. This is so real, but it must be a dream. It must be.

Reaching the matches from his pocket, he struck one. It did very little to illumine the darkness. "God, but it's dark," he said.

"A fact so dread," the rabbit said, "extinguishes all hope."

"Wha . . . ?" Carpenter dropped the match and it went out. "You startled me," he said, striking another match, holding it in the direction of the voice. The rabbit's face looked oddly menacing there in the wavery light of the match. The ears looked almost hornlike, the eyes and nose appeared blood-colored instead of pink. The rabbit's teeth were almost in Carpenter's face. They looked as large and firm as tombstones.

"Now listen, you," Carpenter found himself saying, but his voice cracked and he never completed the sentence. Strong hands grasped him. Two on his left arm, two on his right. It was impossible for him to draw the revolver, and of course he dropped the match.

The rabbit said from the darkness, "Bring him."

The hands gripped Carpenter tighter, carried him forward. Eventually they pulled him out of the gloom and into silvery moonlight. Great stones stood before him, formed a ring. In the center of the massive circle was a long table with chairs—lots of chairs. The table was set with cups, dishes and pouring vessels.

"Stonehenge," Carpenter said. "And the tea party."

"Tea?" came a voice to his left.

Carpenter turned to look at his captors. The one on his left was wearing an outrageously tall top hat. It was the Mad Hatter. On his right, clenching his arm with viselike paws, was the Dormouse.

"You're characters in ALICE IN WONDERLAND. I don't understand," Carpenter said.

"Then you shouldn't talk," said the Hatter.

"This can't be real," Carpenter said. "It has to be a dream."

"The two are much of a muchness," the Hatter explained.

With the rabbit hopping before them, they led Carpenter to one of the upright stones. The Hatter produced from his hat an impossible length of rope, and he and the Dormouse bound Carpenter mummy-wrap tight to the stone. Carpenter could not free himself no matter how hard he struggled, let alone reach the revolver in his coat pocket.

"Why?" Carpenter asked. "Why?"

"Why?" said the rabbit, checking his watch. "Why because it is almost time, and you, my friend, are the much-honored guest." The rabbit lifted his head to the stars, as did the Hatter and the Dormouse, and scrutinized the heavens.

Out beyond the ring of stones there was an uncanny darkness. Carpenter thought he could see eyes there, growing more numerous by the moment, collecting in droves. In one spot, like a moon that had come off its hinge, hung a huge, white Cheshire Cat smile.

The rabbit lowered his head, put his watch back in place. He smiled at Carpenter. Those teeth seemed suddenly very ugly. They reminded Carpenter of nothing less than two huge grinding stones.

"Help me, White Rabbit," Carpenter said. "I've done you no harm. You wouldn't hurt me, would you? Rabbits are by nature gentle and timid creatures."

The rabbit held up one finger. (Odd, thought Carpenter, he had not noticed that the fingers were clawed before.) Then the rabbit began a rhyme.

> "How cheerfully he seems to grin,
>   How neatly spreads his claws,
>   And welcomes little fishes in
>   With gently smiling jaws!"

The rabbit lowered his hand. His pink eyes went deathly dark and cold, like two bright stars that had suddenly gone nova. Slowly, the rabbit walked toward Carpenter. Somewhere, from the darkness beyond the stone ring, came the fluting of pipes, the slow cadence of drums.

Carpenter struggled against the ropes, but to no avail. "God, it's not a dream. It's real!"

"Is it?" said the rabbit.

"A dream? Then it's a dream?"

"It is? My goodness, is it now? Did I say that?"

"You're out of Lewis Carroll's imagination, for Christ's sake!" Carpenter screamed as tears began to run down his cheeks.

"Carroll was such a romanticist," the rabbit said. "He could take the coldest truth and turn it into something sugar-cone sweet. Just refused to see things as they are, you see. Made them out to be fairy tales. A very reprehensible thing for a journalist to do."

The rabbit was very close now, and there was nothing

cute about the way he looked, about those skull-socket eyes, those ugly teeth. Carpenter could smell the sourness of the rabbit's breath, a smell like decaying meat.

"Do not the Japanese say," the rabbit said slowly, "that we only live twice. Once in life and once in our dreams?" He smiled broadly. There seemed to be an endless supply of teeth. "Tonight we kill two birds with one stone."

"Jesus Christ!"

"Yes, yes, indeedy. A very solid fact of Christianity's belief is suffering. Remember Jesus on the cross? Stretched out there for all to see, suffering for redemption. Christianity tells us that if we suffer enough we get a prize, yes indeedy. Are you ready for your prize?"

"You're mad!"

The flutes had risen in tempo; the drums beat in a heart-throb sort of way.

The Hatter said, "It really is time, sir."

"Is it now?" the rabbit said, taking out his watch and examining the face in the moonlight. "Why it is. Quite time, quite."

Carpenter began to laugh hysterically. Tears glistened on his cheeks. "This is crazy! You can't hurt me. You're a dream. You're the frigging White Rabbit in ALICE IN WONDERLAND. You're a dream. I'll wake up!"

"Oh," said the rabbit, looking puzzled, and with surprising deftness, produced from his waistcoat pocket a sharp-bladed knife. "Will you?"

And he cut Carpenter's throat.

Then they all sat down to the feast.

The Dump

I have a soft spot in my heart—or maybe it's my head—for this one, though I hated it when I wrote it. It's a simple little Fred Brown/Robert Bloch sort of story, and it was the result of a popcorn dream, as well as the fact that I was listening to a lot of old radio shows my friend Jeff Banks had loaned me.

About the popcorn dreams. The nuttiness in many of my stories, especially stories of this period, was the result of popcorn. I avoid the stuff most of the time, but when the urge hits, or when the bank account looks low, my wife makes up a huge batch. Her popcorn is the only popcorn that does it to me. She has her own special method of popping it up, and I tend to overeat. I go to bed. I have weird dreams. I get up and write the dreams and sell them. So far, every popcorn dream I've written down—a few were just too nonsensical—has sold. I guess it could be said I owe my career to my wife and her popcorn.

Radio shows. Bloch. Brown. Popcorn dreams. It all came together. I woke up in the middle of the night and wrote this story down. (I seldom do any writing in the middle of the night by the way, but then I was working full time and wrote when I could manage it.) When I finished, I thought it was, to put it mildly, dumb. I didn't even make a copy. I folded it immediately, put it in an envelope so I wouldn't change my mind, went back to bed, and next day mailed it off to the

*then new ROD SERLING'S TWILIGHT ZONE MAGAZINE, a magazine
I badly wanted to appear in.*

*More I thought about the story, dumber I felt. Boy was I
an idiot, and I didn't even have a copy of the story to look
over and see how big an idiot I was.*

*Couple of days later, one night actually, Ted Klein, then
editor of TWILIGHT ZONE MAGAZINE, phoned to say he loved it
and wanted to buy it for the magazine. Later it appeared in
BEST OF THE TWILIGHT ZONE, a magazine anthology. I suddenly
began to like it better.*

For Ted Klein

Me, I like it here just fine. Don't see no call for me to
move on. Dump's been my home nigh on twenty years, and
I don't think no high-falutin' city sanitation law should
make me have to pack up and move on. If I'm gonna work
here, I ought to be able to live here.

Me and Otto . . . where is that sucker anyway? I let him
wander about some on Sundays. Rest of the time I keep him
chained inside the hut there, out of sight. Wouldn't want
him bitin' folks.

Well, as I was sayin', the dump's my home. Best damn
home I ever had. I'm not a college man, but I got some
education. I read a lot. Ought to look inside that shack and
see my bookshelves. I may be a dump-yard supervisor, but
I'm no fool.

Besides, there's more to this dump than meets the eye.

'Scuse me. Otto! Otto. Here, boy. Dadburn his hide, he's
gotten bad about not comin' when I call.

Now, I was sayin' about the dump. There's more here
than meets the eye. You ever thought about all that garbage,
boy? They bring anything and everything here, and I 'doze
her under. There's animal bodies—that's one of the things
that interests old Otto—paint cans, all manner of chemical

containers, lumber, straw, brush, you name it. I 'doze all that stuff under and it heats up. Why, if you could put a thermometer under that earth, check the heat that stuff puts out while it's breakin' down and turnin' to compost, it would be up *there*, boy, way up *there*. Sometimes over a hundred degrees. I've plowed that stuff open and seen the steam flow out of there like a cloud. Could feel the heat of it. It was like bein' in one of them fancy baths. Saunas, they call 'em. Hot, boy, real hot.

Now you think about it. All that heat. All those chemicals and dead bodies and such. Makes an awful mess, a weird blend of nature's refuse. Real weird. And with all that incubatin' heat . . . Well, you consider it.

I'll tell you somethin' I ain't told nobody else. Somethin' that happened to me a couple years ago.

One night me and Pearly, that was a friend of mine, and we called him that on account of he had the whitest teeth you ever seen. Darn things looked *painted* they were so white . . . Let's see, now where was I? Oh, yeah, yeah, me and Pearly. Well, we were sittin' around out here one night shootin' the breeze, you know, sharin' a pint. Pearly, he used to come around from time to time and we'd always split a bottle. He used to be a legit, old-time hobo. Rode the rails all over this country. Why, I reckon he was goin' on seventy years if not better, but he acted twenty years younger.

He'd come around and we'd talk and sit and snort and roll us some of that Prince Albert, which we'd smoke. We had some good laughs, we did, and I miss old Pearly sometimes.

So that night we let the bottle leak out pretty good, and Pearly, he's tellin' me about this time down in Texas in a boxcar with a river trash whore, and he stops in midsentence, right at the good part, and says: "You hear that?"

I said, "I don't hear nothin'. Go on with your story."

He nodded and told the tale, and I laughed, and he

laughed. He could laugh better at his own stories and jokes than anyone I'd ever seen.

After a bit Pearly gets up and walks out beyond the firelight to relieve himself, you know. And he comes back right quick, zippin' his fly, and walkin' as fast as them old stiff legs of his will take him.

"There's somethin' out there," he says.

"Sure," I say. "Armadillos, coons, possums, maybe a stray dog."

"No," he says. "Something else."

"Awww."

"I been a lot of places, boy," he says—he always called me boy on account of I was twenty years younger than he was—"and I'm used to hearin' critters walk about. That don't sound like no damn possum or stray dog to me. Somethin' bigger."

I start to tell him that he's full of it, you know—and then I hear it too. And a stench like you wouldn't believe floats into camp here. A stench like a grave opened on a decomposin' body, one full of maggots and the smell of earth and death. It was so strong I got a little sick, what with all the rotgut in me.

Pearly says, "You hear it?"

And I did. It was the sound of somethin' heavy, crunchin' down that garbage out there, movin' closer and closer to the camp, like it was afeared of the fire, you know.

I got the heebie-jeebies, and I went into the hut there and got my double-barrel. When I came out Pearly had pulled a little old thirty-two Colt out of his waistband and a brand from the fire, and he was headin' out there in the dark.

"Wait a minute," I called.

"You just stay put, boy. I'll see to this, and I'll see that whatever it is gets a hole in it. Maybe six."

So I waited. The wind picked up and that horrible stench drifted in again, very strong this time. Strong enough so I puked up that hooch I'd drunk. And then suddenly from the dark, while I'm leanin' over throwin' my guts out on the ground, I hear a shot. Another one. Another.

I got up and started callin' for Pearly.

"Stay the hell where you are," he called. "I'm comin' back." Another shot, and then Pearly seemed to fold out of the darkness and come into the light of the fire.

"What is it, Pearly?" I said. "What is it?"

Pearly's face was as white as his teeth. He shook his head. "Ain't never seen nothin' like it . . . Listen, boy, we got to get the hell out of Dodge. That sucker, it's—" He let his voice trail off, and he looked toward the darkness beyond the firelight.

"Come on, Pearly, what is it?"

"I tell you, I don't know. I couldn't see real good with that there firebrand, and it went out before too long. I heard it down there crunchin' around, over there by that big hill of garbage."

I nodded. That was a pile I'd had heaped up with dirt for a long time. I intended to break it open next time I 'dozed, push some new stuff in with it.

"It—it was comin' out of that pile," Pearly said. "It was wrigglin' like a great gray worm, but . . . there were legs all over it. Fuzzy legs. And the body—it was jelly-like. Lumber, fence wire, and all manner of crap was stickin' out of it, stickin' out of it like it belonged there, just as natural as a shell on a turtle's back or the whiskers on a cougar's face. It had a mouth, a big mouth, like a railway tunnel, and what looked like teeth . . . But the brand went out then. I fired some shots. It was still wrigglin' out of that garbage heap. It was too dark to stay there—"

He cut in midsentence. The smell was strong now, solid as a wall of bricks.

"It's movin' into camp," I said.

"Must've come from all that garbage," Pearly said. "Must've been born in all that heat and slime."

"Or come up from the center of the earth," I said, though I figured Pearly was a mite near closer to right.

Pearly put some fresh loads in his revolver. "This is all I got," he said.

"I want to see it eat buckshot," I said.

Then we heard it. Very loud, crunchin' down those mounds of garbage like they was peanut hulls. And then there was silence.

Pearly, he moved back a few steps from the double-barrel toward the shack. I aimed the double-barrel toward the dark.

Silence went on for a while. Why, you could've heard yourself blink. But I wasn't blinkin'. I was a-watchin' out for that critter.

Then I heard it—but it was behind me! I turned just in time to see a fuzzy-like tentacle slither out from behind the shack and grab old Pearly. He screamed, and the gun fell out of his hand. And from the shadows a head showed. A huge, wormlike head with slitted eyes and a mouth large enough to swallow a man. Which is what it did. Pearly didn't make that thing two gulps. Wasn't nothin' left of him but a scrap of flesh hangin' on the thing's teeth.

I emptied a load of buckshot in it, slammed the gun open and loaded her again. By that time it was gone. I could hear it crashin' off in the dark.

I got the keys to the 'dozer and walked around back of the shack on tiptoe. It didn't come out of the dark after me. I cranked the 'dozer, turned on the spotlights, and went out there after it.

It didn't take long to find it. It was movin' across the dump like a snake, slitherin' and a-loopin' as fast as it could go—which wasn't too fast right then. It had a lump in its belly, an undigested lump . . . Poor old Pearly!

I ran it down, pinned it to the chain-link fence on the far

side of the dump, and used my 'dozer blade to mash it up against it. I was just fixin' to gun the motor and cut that sucker's head off when I changed my mind.

Its head was stickin' up over the blade, those slitted eyes lookin' at me . . . and there, buried in that wormlike face, was the face of a puppy. You get a lot of them here. Well, it was alive now. Head was still mashed in like it was the first time I saw it, but it was movin'. The head was wrigglin' right there in the center of that worm's head.

I took a chance and backed off from that thing. I dropped to the ground and didn't move. I flashed the lights over it.

Pearly was seepin' out of that thing. I don't know how else to describe it, but he seemed to be driftin' out of that jelly-like hide; and when his face and body were halfway out of it, he stopped movin' and just hung there. I realized somethin' then. It was not only created by the garbage and the heat—it lived off of it, and whatever became its food became a part of it. That puppy and old Pearly were now a part of it.

Now don't misunderstand me. Pearly, he didn't know nothin' about it. He was alive, in a fashion, he moved and squirmed, but like that puppy, he no longer thought. He was just a hair on that thing's body. Same as the lumber and wire and such that stuck out of it.

And the beast—well, it wasn't too hard to tame. I named it Otto. It ain't no trouble at all. Gettin' so it don't come when I call, but that's on account of I ain't had nothin' to reward it with, until you showed up. Before that, I had to kind of help it root dead critters out of the heaps . . . Sit down! I've got Pearly's thirty-two here, and if you move I'll plug you.

Oh, here comes Otto now.

God of the Razor

In 1980, while holding down a full-time job, I began a novel called THE NIGHT OF THE GOBLINS. I had just written ACT OF LOVE and DEAD IN THE WEST in the same year! Not to mention numerous other things. (God, how did I do it?) and I thought it might be nice to try and write a novel proposal—fifty pages and an outline—and try to sell from that.

I wrote the proposal, sent it to my then incompetent and highly irritable agent, and waited. ACT OF LOVE sold before the proposal went out, I believe, then THE NIGHT OF THE GOBLINS went to the same publisher. They thought it was too violent, too strange, and basically, they didn't understand it.

I thought, gee, what's to understand?

I finished the novel in 1982 in a four-month blitz, sent it to my new agent, and he said it didn't fit in any box he could find. It wasn't horror. It wasn't mystery. It wasn't suspense. It wasn't exactly mainstream.

I told him thank you, fired him, marketed the novel around, got the most savage rejects you could imagine, none of them really complaints about the writing, but complaints about the fact that I was trying to write something that shouldn't be talked about. Some of the written rejects practically stuttered.

At least they were paying attention. That was a good sign.

I put the novel away and now and then, assuming it was

*never going to sell, I borrowed from it. I took a portion out
of it, revised it, reslanted it, and came up with this story,
"God of the Razor." I felt I could at least make some profit
out of the time I had invested in the book.*

Nope. No one wanted the short story.

Until Peggy Nadramia at GRUE bought it. Thanks, Peggy.

*The story was later picked up for THE SECOND BLACK LIZARD
ANTHOLOGY OF CRIME FICTION and a mystery best-of-the-year
volume as well. Editors who rejected it the first time out,
and don't remember they did, love to tell me how much they
like it. Uh huh.*

*By the way, the book it was stolen and revised from, as
were a number of other stories, did sell and came out in
1987, five years after it was finished, seven years after it
was conceived. The title was changed. It was called THE
NIGHTRUNNERS.*

                For Ray Puechner and Ardath Mayhar

Richards arrived at the house about eight.

The moon was full and it was a very bright night, in spite
of occasional cloud cover; bright enough that he could get a
good look at the place. It was just as the owner had
described it. Run down. Old. And very ugly.

The style was sort of gothic, sort of plantation, sort of
cracker box. Like maybe the architect had been unable to
decide on a game plan, or had been drunkenly in love with
impossible angles.

Digging the key loaned him from his pocket, he hoped
this would turn out worth the trip. More than once his search
for antiques had turned into a wild goose chase. And this
time, it was really a long shot. The owner, a sick old man
named Klein, hadn't been inside the house in twenty years.
A lot of things could happen to antiques in that time, even
if the place was locked and boarded up. Theft. Insects. Rats.

Leaks. Any one of those, or a combination of, could turn the finest of furniture into rubble and sawdust in no time. But it was worth the gamble. On occasion, his luck had been phenomenal.

As a thick, dark cloud rolled across the moon, Richards, guided by his flashlight, mounted the rickety porch, squeaked the screen and groaned the door open.

Inside, he flashed the light around. Dust and darkness seemed to crawl in there until the cloud passed and the lunar light fell through the boarded windows in a speckled and slatted design akin to camouflaged netting. In places, Richards could see that the wallpaper had fallen from the wall in big sheets that dangled halfway down to the floor like the drooping branches of weeping willows.

To his left was a wide, spiraling staircase, and following its ascent with his light, he could see there were places where the railing hung brokenly askew.

Directly across from this was a door. A narrow, recessed one. As there was nothing in the present room to command his attention, he decided to begin his investigation there. It was as good a place as any.

Using his flashlight to bat his way through a skin of cobwebs, he went over to the door and opened it. Cold air embraced him, brought with it a sour smell, like a freezer full of ruined meat. It was almost enough to turn Richards' stomach, and for a moment he started to close the door and forget it. But an image of wall-to-wall antiques clustered in the shadows came to mind, and he pushed forward, determined. If he were going to go to all the trouble to get the key and drive away out here in search of old furniture to buy, then he ought to make sure he had a good look, smell or no smell.

Using his flash, and helped by the moonlight, he could tell that he had discovered a basement. The steps leading down into it looked aged and precarious, and the floor appeared oddly glass-like in the beam of his light.

So he could examine every nook and cranny of the basement, Richards decided to descend the stairs. He put one foot carefully on the first step, and slowly settled his weight on it. Nothing collapsed. He went down three more steps, cautiously, and though they moaned and squeaked, they held.

When Richards reached the sixth step, for some reason he could not define, he felt oddly uncomfortable, had a chill. It was as if someone with ice-cold water in their kidneys had taken a piss down the back of his coat collar.

Now he could see that the floor was not glassy at all. In fact, the floor was not visible. The reason it had looked glassy from above was because it was flooded with water. From the overall size of the basement, Richards determined that the water was most likely six or seven feet deep. Maybe more.

There was movement at the edge of Richards' flashlight beam, and he followed it. A huge rat was swimming away from him, pushing something before it; an old partially deflated volleyball perhaps. He could not tell for sure. Nor could he decide if the rat was trying to mount the object or bite it.

And he didn't care. Two things that gave him the willies were rats and water, and here were both. To make it worse, the rats were the biggest he'd ever seen, and the water was the dirtiest imaginable. It looked to have a lot of oil and sludge mixed in with it, as well as being stagnant.

It grew darker, and Richards realized the moon had been hazed by a cloud again. He let that be his signal. There was nothing more to see here, so he turned and started up. Stopped. The very large shape of a man filled the doorway.

Richards jerked the light up, saw that the shadows had been playing tricks on him. The man was not as large as he'd first thought. And he wasn't wearing a hat. He had been certain before that he was, but he could see now that he was mistaken. The fellow was bareheaded, and his features, though youthful, were undistinguished; any character he might have had seemed to retreat into the flesh of his face or find sanctuary within the dark folds of his shaggy hair. As he lowered the light, Richards thought he saw the wink of braces on the young man's teeth.

"Basements aren't worth a damn in this part of the country," the young man said. "Must have been some Yankees come down here and built this. Someone who didn't know about the water table, the weather and all."

"I didn't know anyone else was here," Richards said. "Klein send you?"

"Don't know a Klein."

"He owns the place. Loaned me a key."

The young man was silent a moment. "Did you know the moon is behind a cloud? A cloud across the moon can change the entire face of the night. Change it the way some people change their clothes, their moods, their expressions."

Richards shifted uncomfortably.

"You know," the young man said. "I couldn't shave this morning."

"Beg pardon?"

"When I tried to put a blade in my razor, I saw that it had an eye on it, and it was blinking at me, very fast. Like this . . . oh, you can't see from down there, can you? Well, it was very fast. I dropped it and it slid along the sink, dove off on the floor, crawled up the side of the bathtub and got in the soap dish. It closed its eye then, but it started mewing like a kitten wanting milk. Ooooowww-waaa, Oooowwwaa, was more the way it sounded really, but it reminded me of a kitten. I knew what it wanted, of course. What it always wants. What all the sharp things want.

"Knowing what it wanted made me sick and I threw up in the toilet. Vomited up a razor blade. It was so fat it might have been pregnant. Its eye was blinking at me as I flushed it. When it was gone the blade in the soap dish started to sing high and silly-like.

"The blade I vomited, I know how it got inside of me." The young man raised his fingers to his throat. "There was a little red mark right here this morning, and it was starting to scab over. One or two of them always find a way in. Sometimes it's nails that get in me. They used to come in through the soles of my feet while I slept, but I stopped that pretty good by wearing my shoes to bed."

In spite of the cool of the basement, Richards had started to sweat. He considered the possibility of rushing the guy or just trying to push past him, but dismissed it. The stairs might be too weak for sudden movement, and maybe the fruitcake might just have his say and go on his way.

"It really doesn't matter how hard I try to trick them," the young man continued, "they always win out in the end. Always."

"I think I'll come up now," Richards said, trying very hard to sound casual.

The young man flexed his legs. The stairs shook and squealed in protest. Richards nearly toppled backward into the water.

"Hey!" Richards yelled.

"Bad shape," the young man said. "Need a lot of work. Rebuilt entirely would be the ticket."

Richards regained both his balance and his composure. He couldn't decide if he was angry or scared, but he wasn't about to move. Going up he had rotten stairs and Mr. Looney Tunes. Behind him he had the rats and water. The proverbial rock and a hard place.

"Maybe it's going to cloud up and rain," the young man said. "What do you think? Will it rain tonight?"

"I don't know," Richards managed.

"Lot of dark clouds floating about. Maybe they're rain clouds. Did I tell you about the God of the Razor? I really meant to. He rules the sharp things. He's the god of those who live by the blade. He was my friend Donny's god. Did you know he was Jack the Ripper's god?"

The young man dipped his hand into his coat pocket, pulled it out quickly and whipped his arm across his body twice, very fast. Richards caught a glimpse of something long and metal in his hand. Even the cloud-veiled moonlight managed to give it a dull, silver spark.

Richards put the light on him again. The young man was holding the object in front of him, as if he wished it to be examined. It was an impossibly large straight razor.

"I got this from Donny," the young man said. "He got it in an old shop somewhere. Gladewater, I think. It comes from a barber kit, and the kit originally came from England. Says so in the case. You should see the handle on this baby. Ivory. With a lot of little designs and symbols carved into it. Donny looked the symbols up. They're geometric patterns used for calling up a demon. Know what else? Jack the Ripper was no surgeon. He was a barber. I know, because Donny got the razor and started having these visions where Jack the Ripper and the God of the Razor came to talk to him. They explained what the razor was for. Donny said the reason they could talk to him was because he tried to shave with the razor and cut himself. The blood on the blade, and those symbols on the handle, they opened the gate. Opened it so the God of the Razor could come and live inside Donny's head. The Ripper told him that the metal in the blade goes all the way back to a sacrificial altar the Druids used."

The young man stopped talking, dropped the blade to his side. He looked over his shoulder. "That cloud is very dark . . . slow moving. I sort of bet on rain." He turned back to Richards. "Did I ask you if you thought it would rain tonight?"

Richards found he couldn't say a word. It was as if his tongue had turned to cork in his mouth. The young man didn't seem to notice or care.

"After Donny had the visions, he just talked and talked about this house. We used to play here when we were kids. Had the boards on the back window rigged so they'd slide like a trap door. They're still that way . . . Donny used to say this house had angles that sharpened the dull edges of your mind. I know what he means now. It is comfortable, don't you think?"

Richards, who was anything but comfortable, said nothing. Just stood very still, sweating, fearing, listening, aiming the light.

"Donny said the angles were honed best during the full moon. I didn't know what he was talking about then. I didn't understand about the sacrifices. Maybe you know about them? Been all over the papers and on the TV. The Decapitator they called him.

"It was Donny doing it, and from the way he started acting, talking about the God of the Razor, Jack the Ripper, this old house and its angles, I got suspicious. He got so he wouldn't even come around near or during a full moon, and when the moon started waning, he was different. Peaceful. I followed him a few times, but didn't have any luck. He drove to the Safeway, left his car there and walked. He was as quick and sneaky as a cat. He'd lose me right off. But then I got to figuring . . . him talking about this old house and all . . . and one full moon I came here and waited for him, and he showed up. You know what he was doing? He was bringing the heads here, tossing them down there in the water like those South American Indians used to toss bodies and stuff in sacrificial pools . . . It's the angles in the house, you see."

Richards had that sensation like ice-cold piss down his collar again, and suddenly he knew what that swimming rat had been pursuing, and what it was trying to do.

"He threw all seven heads down there, I figure," the young man said. "I saw him toss one." He pointed with the razor. "He was standing about where you are now when he did it. When he turned and saw me, he ran up after me. I froze, couldn't move a muscle. Every step he took, closer he got to me, the stranger he looked . . . he slashed me with the razor, across the chest, real deep. I fell down and he stood over me, the razor cocked," the young man cocked the razor to show Richards. "I think I screamed. But he didn't cut me again. It was like the rest of him was warring with the razor in his hand. He stood up, and walking stiff as one of those wind-up toy soldiers, he went back down the stairs, stood about where you are now, looked up at me, and drew that razor straight across his throat so hard and deep he damn near cut his head off. He fell back in the water there, sunk like an anvil. The razor landed on the last step.

"Wasn't any use; I tried to get him out of there, but he was gone, like he'd never been. I couldn't see a ripple. But the razor was lying there and I could hear it. Hear it sucking up Donny's blood like a kid sucking the sweet out of a sucker. Pretty soon there wasn't a drop of blood on it . . . I picked it up . . . so shiny, so damned shiny. I came upstairs, passed out on the floor from the loss of blood.

"At first I thought I was dreaming, or maybe delirious, because I was lying at the end of this dark alley between these trashcans with my back against the wall. There were legs sticking out of the trashcans, like tossed mannikins. Only they weren't mannikins. There were razor blades and nails sticking out of the soles of the feet and blood was running down the ankles and legs, swirling so that they looked like giant peppermint sticks. Then I heard a noise like someone trying to dribble a medicine ball across a hardwood floor. *Plop, plop, plop.* And then I saw the God of the Razor.

"First there's nothing in front of me but stewing shadows, and the next instant he's there. Tall and black . . . not Negro . . . but black like obsidian rock. Had eyes like smashed windshield glass and teeth like polished stickpins. Was wearing a top hat with this shiny band made out of chrome razor blades. His coat and pants looked like they were made out of human flesh, and sticking out of the pockets of his coat were gnawed fingers, like after dinner treats. And he had this big old turnip pocket watch dangling out of his pants pocket on a strand of gut. The watch swung between his legs as he walked. And that plopping sound, know what that was? His shoes. He had these tiny, tiny feet and they were fitted right into the mouths of these human heads. One of the heads was a woman's and it dragged long black hair behind it when the God walked.

"Kept telling myself to wake up. But I couldn't. The God pulled this chair out of nowhere—it was made out of leg bones and the seat looked like scraps of flesh and hunks of hair—and he sat down, crossed his legs and dangled one of those ragged-head shoes in my face. Next thing he does is whip this ventriloquist dummy out of the air, and it looked like Donny, and was dressed like Donny had been last time I'd seen him, down there on the stair. The God put the dummy on his knee and Donny opened his eyes and spoke. 'Hey, buddy boy,' he said, 'how goes it? What do you think of the razor's bite? You see, pal, if you don't die from it, it's like a vampire's bite. Get my drift? You got to keep passing it on. The sharp things will tell you when, and if you don't want to do it, they'll bother you until you do, or you slice yourself bad enough to come over here on the Darkside with me and Jack and the others. Well, got to go back now, join the gang. Be talking with you real soon, moving into your head.'

"Then he just sort of went limp on the God's knee, and the God took off his hat and he had this zipper running along the middle of his bald head. A goddamned zipper! He pulled it open. Smoke and fire and noises like screaming and car wrecks happening came out of there. He picked up the Donny dummy, which was real small now, and tossed him into the hole in his head way you'd toss a treat into a Great Dane's mouth. Then he zipped up again and put on his hat. Never said a word. But he leaned forward and held his turnip watch so I could see it. The watch hands were skeleton fingers, and there was a face in there, pressing its nose in little smudged circles against the glass, and though I couldn't hear it, the face had its mouth open and it was screaming, and *that face was mine*. Then the God and the alley and the legs in the trashcans were gone. And so was the cut on my chest. Healed completely. Not even a mark.

"I left out of there and didn't tell a soul. And Donny, just like he said, came to live in my head, and the razor started singing to me nights, probably a song sort of like those sirens sang for that Ulysses fellow. And come near and on the full moon, the blades act up, mew and get inside of me. Then I know what I need to do . . . I did it tonight. Maybe if it had rained I wouldn't have had to do it . . . but it was clear enough for me to be busy."

The young man stopped talking, turned, stepped inside the house, out of sight. Richards sighed, but his relief was short-lived. The young man returned and came down a couple of steps. In one hand, by the long blond hair, he was holding a teenaged girl's head. The other clutched the razor.

The cloud veil fell away from the moon, and it became quite bright.

The young man, with a flick of his wrist, tossed the head at Richards, striking him in the chest, causing him to drop the light. The head bounced between Richards' legs and into the water with a flat splash.

"Listen . . ." Richards started, but anything he might have said aged, died and turned to dust in his mouth.

Fully outlined in the moonlight, the young man started down the steps, holding the razor before him like a battle flag.

Richards blinked. For a moment it looked as if the guy were wearing a . . . He was wearing a hat. A tall, black one with a shiny, metal band. And he was much larger now, and between his lips was a shimmer of wet, silver teeth like thirty-two polished stickpins.

Plop, plop came the sound of his feet on the steps, and in the lower and deeper shadows of the stairs, it looked as if the young man had not only grown in size and found a hat, but had darkened his face and stomped his feet into pumpkins . . . But one of the pumpkins streamed long, dark hair.

Plop, plop . . . Richards screamed and the sound of it rebounded against the basement walls like a superball.

Shattered starlight eyes beneath the hat. A Cheshire smile of argentine needles in a carbon face. A big dark hand holding the razor, whipping it back and forth like a lion's talon snatching at warm, soft prey.

Swish, swish, swish.

Richards' scream was dying in his throat, if not in the echoing basement, when the razor flashed for him. He avoided it by stepping briskly backward. His foot went underwater, but found a step there. Momentarily. The rotting wood gave way, twisted his ankle, sent him plunging into the cold, foul wetness.

Just before his eyes, like portholes on a sinking ship, were covered by the liquid darkness, he saw the God of the Razor—now manifest in all his horrid form—lift a splitting head shoe and step into the water after him.

Richards torqued his body, swam long, hard strokes, coasted bottom; his hand touched something cold and clammy down there and a piece of it came away in his fingers.

Flipping it from him with a fan of his hand, he fought his way to the surface and broke water as the blonde girl's head bobbed in front of him, two rat passengers aboard, gnawing viciously at the eye sockets.

Suddenly, the girl's head rose, perched on the crown of the tall hat of the God of the Razor, then it tumbled off, rats and all, into the greasy water.

Now there was the jet face of the God of the Razor and his mouth was open and the teeth blinked briefly before the lips drew tight, and the other hand, like an eggplant sprouting fingers, clutched Richards' coat collar and plucked him forward and Richards—the charnel breath of the God in his face, the sight of the lips slashing wide to once again reveal brilliant dental grill work—went limp as a pelt. And the God raised the razor to strike.

And the moon tumbled behind a thick, dark cloud.

White face, shaggy hair, no hat, a fading glint of silver teeth . . . the young man holding the razor, clutching Richards' coat collar.

The juice back in his heart, Richards knocked the man's hand free, and the guy went under. Came up thrashing. Went under again. And when he rose this time, the razor was frantically flaying the air.

"Can't swim," he bellowed, "can't—" Under he went, and this time he did not come up. But Richards felt something touch his foot from below. He kicked out savagely, dog paddling wildly all the while. Then the touch was gone and the sloshing water went immediately calm.

Richards swam toward the broken stairway, tried to ignore the blond head that lurched by, now manned by a four-rat crew. He got hold of the loose, dangling stair rail and began to pull himself up. The old board screeched on its loosening nail, but held until Richards gained a hand on the door ledge, then it gave way with a groan and went to join the rest of the rotting lumber, the heads, the bodies, the faded stigmata of the God of the Razor.

Pulling himself up, Richards crawled into the room on his hands and knees, rolled over on his back . . . and something flashed between his legs . . . It was the razor. It was stuck to the bottom of his shoe . . . That had been the touch he had felt from below; the young guy still trying to cut him, or perhaps accidentally striking him during his desperate thrashings to regain the surface.

Sitting up, Richards took hold of the ivory handle and freed the blade. He got to his feet and stumbled toward the door. His ankle and foot hurt like hell where the step had given way beneath him, hurt him so badly he could hardly walk.

Then he felt the sticky, warm wetness oozing out of his foot to join the cold water in his shoe, and he knew that he had been cut by the razor.

But then he wasn't thinking anymore. He wasn't hurting anymore. The moon rolled out from behind a cloud like a colorless eye and he just stood there looking at his shadow on the lawn. The shadow of an impossibly large man wearing a top hat and balls on his feet, holding a monstrous razor in his hand.

Chompers

I developed a sort of free-wheeling nuttiness for the stories I wrote for TWILIGHT ZONE MAGAZINE, and it became something of a temporary trademark. So much, in fact, that when I tried to sell a story to TZ, or anywhere else, that wasn't of that sort, it came back immediately. I eventually broke that mold, showed that I could and liked to do a variety of things, but for a time in my career this was the sort of thing I was known for.

This nuttiness was often derived through the overeating of popcorn, as I've previously explained. This story came one night after eating popcorn and watching a movie, and afterwards the news, where one of the commercials was for a denture product, and then later there was something about Gandhi, though I don't remember exactly what. Whatever, I remember noticing that dude had some serious dental problems.

I went to bed with teeth on my mind, woke up in the middle of the night and hammered out the following story in about twenty minutes, revised it in about the same time the next day and sent it to Ted Klein at TZ. He changed my title "False Teeth" to "Chompers" and it appeared with a wonderful illustration by Randy Jones. It's fluff, but it's fun fluff.

Gee, this intro is almost longer than the story.

For Steve Mertz

Old Maude, who lived in alleys, combed trash cans, and picked rags, found the false teeth in a puddle of blood back of Denny's. Obvious thing was that there had been a mugging, and some unfortunate who'd been wandering around out back had gotten his or her brains beaten out, and then hauled off somewhere for who knows what.

But the teeth, which had probably hopped from the victim's mouth like some kind of frightened animal, still remained, and the blood they lay in was testimony to the terrible event.

Maude picked them up, looked at them. Besides the blood there were some pretty nasty coffee stains on the rear molars and what looked to be a smidgen of cherry pie. One thing Maude could spot and tell with an amazing degree of accuracy was a stain or a food dollop. Cruise alleyways and dig in trash cans most of your life, and you get skilled.

Now, Maude was a practical old girl, and, as she had about as many teeth in her head as a pomegranate, she wiped the blood off on her dress—high fashion circa 1920—and put those suckers right square in her gummy little mouth. Somehow it seemed like the proper thing to do.

Perfect fit. Couldn't have been any better than if they'd been made for her. She got the old, blackened lettuce head out of her carpet bag—she'd found the lettuce with a half a tomato back of Burger King—and gave that vegetable a chomp. Sounded like the dropping of a guillotine as those teeth snapped into the lettuce and then ground it to smithereens.

Man that was good for a change, thought Maude, to be able to go at your food like a pig to trough. Gumming your vittles gets old.

The teeth seemed a little tighter in her mouth than a while ago, but Maude felt certain that after a time she'd get used to them. It was sad about the poor soul that had lost them, but that person's bad luck was her fortune.

Maude started toward the doorway she called home, and by the time she'd gone a block she found that she was really hungry, which surprised her. Not an hour back she'd eaten half a hamburger out of a Burger King trash can, three greasy fries, and half an apple pie. But, boy howdy, did she want to chow down now. She felt like she could eat anything.

She got the tomato half out of her bag, along with everything else in there that looked edible, and began to eat.

More she ate, hungrier she got. Pretty soon she was out of goodies, and the sidewalk and the street started looking to her like the bottom of a dinner plate that ought to be filled. God, but her belly burned. It was as if she'd never eaten and had suddenly become aware of the need.

She ground her big teeth and walked on. Half a block later she spotted a big alleycat hanging head down over the lip of a trash can, pawing for something to eat, and ummm, ummm, ummm, but that cat looked tasty as a Dunkin' Donut.

Chased that rascal for three blocks, but didn't catch it. It pulled a fade-out on her in a dark alley.

Disgusted, but still very, very hungry, Maude left the alley thinking: Chow, need me some chow.

Beat cop O'Hara was twirling his nightstick when he saw her nibbling the paint off a rusty old streetlamp. It was an old woman with a prune face, and when he came up she stopped nibbling and looked at him. She had the biggest, shiniest pair of choppers he had ever seen. They stuck out from between her lips like a gator's teeth, and in the light of the streetlamp, even as he watched, he thought for a moment that he had seen them grow. And, by golly, they looked pointed now.

O'Hara had walked his beat for twenty years, and he was

used to eccentrics and weird getups, but there was something particularly weird about this one.

The old woman *smiled* at him.

Man, there were a lot of teeth there. (More than a while ago?) O'Hara thought: Now that's a crazy thing to think.

He was about six feet from her when she jumped him, teeth gnashing, clicking together like a hundred cold Eskimo knees. They caught his shirt sleeve and ripped it off; the cloth disappeared between those teeth fast as a waiter's tip.

O'Hara struck at her with his nightstick, but she caught that in her mouth, and those teeth of hers began to rattle and snap like a pound full of rabid dogs. Wasn't nothing left of that stick but toothpicks.

He pulled his revolver, but she ate that too. Then she ate O'Hara, didn't even leave a shoe.

Little later on she ate a kid on a bicycle—the bicycle too—and hit up a black hooker for dessert. But that didn't satisfy her. She was still hungry, and, worse yet, the pickings had gotten lean.

Long about midnight, this part of the city went dead except for a bum or two, and she ate them. She kept thinking that if she could get across town to Forty-second Street, she could have her fill of hookers, kids, pimps, and heroin addicts. It'd be a regular buffet-style dinner.

But that was such a long ways off and she was *sooooo hungry*. And those damn teeth were so big now she felt as if she needed a neck brace just to hold her head up.

She started walking fast, and when she was about six blocks away from the smorgasbord of Forty-second, her mouth started watering like Niagara Falls.

Suddenly she had an attack. She had to eat NOW—as in "a while ago." *Immediately.*

Halfway up her arm, she tried to stop. But my, was that tasty. Those teeth went to work, a-chomping and a-rending, and pretty soon they were as big as a bear trap, snapping flesh like it was chewing gum.

Wasn't nothing left of Maude but a puddle of blood by the time the teeth fell to the sidewalk, rapidly shrinking back to normal size.

Harry, high on life and high on wine, wobbled down the sidewalk, dangling left, dangling right. It was a wonder he didn't fall down.

He saw the teeth lying in a puddle of blood, and having no choppers of his own—the tooth fairy had them all—he decided, what the hell, what can it hurt? Besides, he felt driven.

Picking up the teeth, wiping them off, he placed them in his mouth.

Perfect fit. Like they were made for him.

He wobbled off, thinking: Man, but I'm hungry; gracious, but I sure could eat.

The Fat Man

I don't remember a damn thing about this one. All I can say is it's obviously a Bradbury influenced story and it takes place in my fictional town of Mud Creek. And, I like it. I suspicion, but can't verify, popcorn had something to do with it.

For Ted Olsen

The Fat Man sat on his porch in his squeaking swing and looked out at late October. Leaves coasted from the trees that grew on either side of the walk, coasted down and scraped the concrete with a dry, husking sound.

He sat there in his swing, pushing one small foot against the porch, making the swing go back and forth; sat there in his faded khaki pants, barefoot, shirtless, his belly hanging way out over his belt, drooping toward his knees.

And just below his belly button, off-center right, was the tattoo. A half-moon, lying on its back, the ends pointing up. A blue tattoo. An obscene tattoo, made obscene by the sagging flesh on which it was sculptured. Flesh that made the Fat Man look like a hippo if a hippo could stand on its hind legs or sit in a swing pushing itself back and forth.

The Fat Man.

Late October.

Cool wind.

Falling leaves.

The Fat Man with the half-moon tattoo off-center beneath his navel.

The Fat Man. Swinging.

Everyone wondered about the Fat Man. He had lived in the little house at the end of Crowler Street for a long time. Forever it seemed. As long as that house had been there (circa 1920), he had been there. No one knew anything else about him. He did not go to town. He did not venture any farther than his front porch, as if his house were an odd-ball ship adrift forever on an endless sea. He had a phone, but no electric lights. He did not use gas and he had no car.

And everyone wondered about the Fat Man.

Did he pay taxes?

Where did he get the money that bought the countless boxes of chicken, pizza, egg foo yung, and hamburgers he ordered by phone; the countless grease-stained boxes that filled the garbage cans he set off the edge of his porch each Tuesday and Thursday for the sanitation men to pick up and empty?

Why didn't he use electric lights?

Why didn't he go to town?

Why did he sit on his porch in his swing looking out at the world smiling dumbly, going in the house only when night came?

And what did he do at night behind those closed doors?

Why did he wear neither shirt nor shoes, summer or dead of winter?

And where in the world—and why—did he get that ugly half-moon tattooed on his stomach?

Whys and whats. Lots of them about the Fat Man. Questions aplenty, answers none.

Everyone wondered about the Fat Man.

But no one wondered as much as Harold and Joe, two

boys who filled their days with comics, creek beds, climbing apple trees, going to school . . . and wondering about the Fat Man.

So one cool night, late October, they crept up to the Fat Man's house, crawling on hands and knees through the not-yet-dead weeds in the empty lot next to the Fat Man's house, and finally through the equally high weeds in the Fat Man's yard.

They lay in the cool, wind-rustled weeds beneath one of the Fat Man's windows and whispered to each other.

"Let's forget it," Harold said.

"Can't. We come this far, and we swore on a dead cat."

"A dead cat don't care."

"A dead cat's sacred, you know that."

"We made that up."

"And because we did that makes it true. A dead cat's sacred."

Harold could not find it in his heart to refute this. They found the dead cat on the street next to the curb the day before, and Joe had said right off that it was sacred. And Harold, without contesting, had agreed.

And how could he disagree? The looks of the cat were hypnotizing. Its little gray body was worm-worked. Its teeth exposed. Its lips were drawn back, black and stiff. All the stuff to draw the eye. All the stuff that made it sacred.

They took the cat over the creek, through the woods and out to the old "Indian" graveyard and placed it on the ground where Joe said an old Caddo Chief was buried. They took the cat and poked its stiff legs into the soft dirt so that it appeared to be running through quicksand.

Joe said, "I pronounce you a sacred cat with powers as long as there's hair on your body and you don't fall over, which ever comes first."

They made an oath on the sacred cat, and the oath was like this: They were going to sneak over to the Fat Man's

house when their parents were asleep, and find out just what
in hell and heaven the Fat Man did. Maybe see him eat so
they could find out how quickly he went through those
boxes and cartons of chicken, pizza, egg foo yung, hamburgers and the like.

Above them candle light flickered through the thin
curtains and window. Joe raised up cautiously for a peek.

Inside he saw the candle residing in a broken dish on an
end-table next to the telephone. And that was it for the Fat
Man's furniture. The rest of the room was filled with food
boxes and cartons, and wading knee-deep in their midst,
was the Fat Man.

The Fat Man had two large trash cans next to him, and he
was bending quite nimbly for a man his size (and as he bent
the fat about his middle made three thick anaconda coils,
one of which was spotted with the blue half-moon tattoo),
picking up the boxes and tossing them in the cans.

Harold raised up for a look.

Soon the cans were stuffed and overflowing and the Fat
Man had cleared a space on the floor. With the handle of a
can in either hand, the Fat Man swung the cans toward the
door, outside and off the edge of the porch.

The Fat Man came back, closed the door, kicked his way
through the containers until he reached the clearing he had
made.

He said in a voice that seemed somewhat distant, and
originating at the pit of his stomach, "Tip, tap, tip tap."
Then his voice turned musical and he began to sing, "Tip,
tap, tip tap."

His bare feet flashed out on the hardwood floor with a
sound not unlike tap shoes or wood clicking against wood,
and the Fat Man kept repeating the line, dancing around and
around, moving light as a ninety-pound ballerina, the
obscene belly swinging left and right to the rhythm of his
song and his fast-moving feet.

"Tip, tap, tip tap."

There was a knock at the door.

The Fat Man stopped dancing, started kicking the boxes aside, making his way to answer the knock.

Joe dropped from the window and edged around the corner of the house and looked at the porch.

A delivery boy stood there with five boxes of pizza stacked neatly on one palm. It was that weird guy from Calo's Pizza. The one with all the personality of a puppet. Or at least that was the way he was these days. Once he had been sort of a joker, but the repetition of pizza to go had choked out and hardened any fun that might have been in him.

The Fat Man's hand came out and took the pizzas. No money was exchanged. The delivery boy went down the steps, clicked down the walk, got in the Volkswagen with Calo's Pizza written on the side, and drove off.

Joe crept back to the window, raised up next to Harold.

The Fat Man put the pizza boxes on the end-table by the phone, opened the top one and took out the pizza, held it balanced on his palm like a droopy painter's palette.

"Tip, tap, tip tap," he sang from somewhere down in his abdomen, then turned, his back to the window. With a sudden movement, he slammed the pizza into his stomach.

"Ahhh," said the Fat Man, and little odd muscles like toy trucks drove up and down his back. His khaki-covered butt perked up and he began to rock on his toes. Fragments of pizza, gooey cheese, sticky sauce and rounds of pepperoni dripped to the floor.

The Fat Man's hand floated out, clutched another box and ripped it open. Out came a pizza, wham, into the stomach, "ah," went the Fat Man, and down dripped more pizza ingredients, and out went the Fat Man's hand once again.

Three pizzas in the stomach.

Now four.

"I don't think I understand all I know about this," Joe whispered.

Five pizzas, and a big, "ahhhhhh," this time.

The fat man leaped, high and pretty, hands extended for a dive, and without a sound he disappeared into the food-stained cartons.

Joe blinked.

Harold blinked.

The Fat Man surfaced. His back humped up first like a rising porpoise, then disappeared. Loops of back popped through the boxes at regular intervals until he reached the far wall.

The Fat Man stood up, bursting cartons around him like scales. He touched the wall with his palm. The wall swung open. Joe and Harold could see light in there and the top of a stairway.

The Fat Man stepped on the stairway, went down. The door closed.

Joe and Harold looked at each other.

"That wall ain't even a foot thick," Harold said. "He can't do that."

"He did," Joe said. "He went right into that wall and down, and you know it because you saw him."

"I think I'll go home now," Harold said.

"You kidding?"

"No, I ain't kidding."

The far wall opened again and out popped the Fat Man, belly greased and stained with pizza.

Joe and Harold watched attentively as he leaped into the boxes, and swam for the clearing. Then, once there, he rose and put a thumb to the candle and put out the light.

He kicked his way through boxes and cartons this time, and his shadowy shape disappeared from the room and into another.

"I'm going to see how he went through the wall," Joe said.

Joe put his hands on the window and pushed. It wasn't locked. It slid up a few inches.

"Don't," Harold whispered, putting his hand on Joe's arm.

"I swore on the dead cat I was going to find out about the Fat Man, and that's what I'm going to do."

Joe shrugged Harold's arm off, pushed the window up higher and climbed through.

Harold swore, but followed.

They went as quietly as they could through the boxes and cartons until they reached the clearing where the pizza glop lay pooled and heaped on the floor. Then they entered the bigger stack of boxes, waded toward the wall. And though they went silently as possible, the cartons still crackled and popped, as if they were trying to call for their master, the Fat Man.

Joe touched the wall with his palm the way the Fat Man had. The wall opened. Joe and Harold crowded against each other and looked down the stairway. It led to a well-lit room below.

Joe went down.

Harold started to say something, knew it was useless. Instead he followed down the stairs.

At the bottom they stood awestruck. It was a workshop of sorts. Tubes and dials stuck out of the walls. Rods of glass were filled with pulsating colored lights. Cables hung on pegs. And there was something else hanging on pegs.

Huge marionettes.

And though they were featureless, hairless and sexless, they looked in form as real as living, breathing people. In fact, put clothes and a face on them and you wouldn't know the difference. Provided they could move and talk, of course.

Harold took hold of the leg of one of the bodies. It felt like wood, but it bent easily. He tied the leg in a knot.

Joe found a table with something heaped on it and covered with black cloth. He whipped off the cloth and said, "Good gracious."

Harold looked.

It was a row of jars, and in the jars, drooping over upright rods, were masks. Masks of people they knew.

Why there was Alice Dunn the Avon Lady. They'd know that wart on her nose anywhere. It fit the grump personality she had these days.

Jerry James the constable. And my, didn't the eyes in his mask look just like his eyes? The way he always looked at them like he was ready to pull his gun and put them under arrest.

May Bloom, the town librarian, who had grown so foul in her old age. No longer willing to help the boys find new versions of King Arthur or order the rest of Edgar Rice Burroughs' Mars series.

And there was the face of the weird guy from Calo's Pizza, Jake was his name . . .

"Now wait a minute," Joe said. "All these people have got something in common. What is it?"

"They're grumps," Harold said.

"Uh huh. What else?"

"I don't know."

"They weren't always grumpy."

"Well, yeah," Harold said.

And Harold thought of how Jake used to kid with him at the pizza place. How the constable had helped him get his kite down from a tree. How Mrs. Bloom had introduced him to Edgar Rice Burroughs, Max Brand, and King Arthur. How Alice Dunn used to make her rounds, and come back special with a gift for him when he was sick.

"There's another thing," Joe said. "Alice Dunn, the

Avon Lady. She always goes door to door, right? So she had to come to the Fat Man's door sometime. And the constable, I bet he came too, on account of all the weird rumors about the Fat Man. Jake, the delivery boy. Mrs. Bloom, who sometimes drives the bookmobile . . ."

"What are you saying?"

"I'm saying, that that little liquid in the bottom of each of these jars looks like blood. I think the Fat Man skinned them, and . . ." Joe looked toward the puppets on the wall, "replaced them with handmade versions."

"Puppets come to life?" Harold said.

"Like Pinocchio," Joe said.

Harold looked at the masks in the jars and suddenly they didn't look so much like masks. He looked at the puppets on the wall and thought he recognized the form of one of them; tall and slightly pudgy with a finger missing on the left hand.

"God, Dad," he said.

"He works for Ma Bell," Joe said. "Repairs lines. And if the Fat Man has phone trouble, and they call out a repairman . . ."

"Don't say it," Harold said.

Joe didn't, but he looked at the row of empty jars behind the row of filled ones.

"What worries me," Joe said, "are the empty jars, and," he turned and pointed to the puppets on the wall, "those two small puppets on the far wall. They look to be about mine and your sizes."

"Oh, they are," said the Fat Man.

Harold shrieked, turned. There at the foot of the stairs stood the Fat Man. And the half-moon tattoo was not a half-moon at all, it was a mouth, and it was speaking to them in the gut-level voice they had heard the Fat Man use to sing.

Joe grabbed up the jar holding Miss Bloom's face and

tossed it at the Fat Man. The Fat Man swept the jar aside and it crashed to the floor; the mask(face) went skidding along on slivers of broken glass.

"Now that's not nice," said the half-moon tattoo, and this time it opened so wide the boys thought they saw something moving in there. "That's my collection."

Joe grabbed another jar, Jerry James this time, tossed it at the Fat Man as he moved lightly and quickly toward them.

Again the Fat Man swatted it aside, and now he was chasing them. Around the table they went, around and around like little Black Sambo being pursued by the tiger.

Harold bolted for the stairs, hit the bottom step, started taking them two at the time.

Joe hit the bottom step.

And the Fat Man grabbed him by the collar.

"Boys, boys," said the mouth in the Fat Man's stomach. "Here now, boys, let's have a little fun."

"Run," yelled Joe. "Get help. He's got me good."

The Fat Man took Joe by the head and stuffed the head into his stomach. The mouth slobbered around Joe's neck.

Harold stood at the top of the stairs dumbfounded. In went Joe, inch by inch. Now only his legs were kicking.

Harold turned, slapped his palm along the wall.

Nothing happened.

Up the stairs came the Fat Man.

Harold glanced back. Only one leg stuck out of the belly now, and it was thrashing. The tennis shoe flew off and slapped against the stairs. Harold could hear a loud gurgling sound coming from the Fat Man's stomach, and a voice saying, "ahhhh, ahhhh."

Halfway up the steps came the Fat Man.

Harold palmed the wall, inch by inch.

Nothing happened.

He jerked a glance back again.

There was a burping sound, and the Fat Man's mouth

opened wide and out flopped Joe's face, skinned, mask-
looking. Harold could also see two large cables inside the
Fat Man's mouth. The cable rolled. The mouth closed.
Taloned, skinny hands stuck out of the blue tattoo and the
fingers wriggled. "Come to Papa," said the voice in the Fat
Man's stomach.

Harold turned, slapped his palm on the wall time and time
again, left and right.

He could hear the Fat Man's tread on the steps right
behind, taking it torturously slow and easy.

The wall opened.

Harold dove into the boxes and cartons and disappeared
beneath them.

The Fat Man leaped high, his dive perfect, his toes
wriggling like stubby, greedy fingers.

Poof, into the boxes.

Harold came up running, kicking boxes aside.

The Fat Man's back, like the fin of a shark, popped the
boxes up. Then he was gone again.

Harold made the clearing in the floor. The house seemed
to be rocking. He turned left toward the door and jerked it
open.

Stepping out on the front porch he froze.

The Fat Man's swing dangled like an empty canary perch,
and the night . . . was different. Thick as chocolate pud-
ding. And the weeds didn't look the same. They looked like
a foamy green sea—putrid sherbet—and the house bobbed
as if it were a cork on the ocean.

Behind Harold the screen door opened. "There you are,
you bad boy, you," said the voice in the belly.

Harold ran and leaped off the porch into the thick, high
weeds, made his way on hands and knees, going almost as
fast as a running dog that way. The ground beneath him
bucked and rolled.

Behind him he heard something hit the weeds but he did

not look back. He kept running on hands and knees for a distance, then he rose to his feet, elbows flying, strides deepening, parting the waist-level foliage like a knife through spoiled cream cheese.

And the grass in front of him opened up. A white face floated into view at belt-level.

The Fat Man. On his knees.

The Fat Man smiled. Skinny, taloned hands stuck out of the blue tattoo and the fingers wiggled.

"Pee-pie," said the Fat Man's belly.

Harold wheeled to the left, tore through the tall weeds yelling. He could see the moon floating in the sky and it looked pale and sick, like a yolkless egg. The houses outlined across the street were in the right place, but they looked off-key, only vaguely reminiscent of how he remembered them. He thought he saw something large and shadowy peek over the top of one of them, but in a blinking of an eye it was gone.

Suddenly the Fat Man was in front of him again.

Harold skidded to a halt.

"You swore on a dead cat," the voice in the belly said, and a little wizened, oily head with bugged-out eyes poked out of the belly and looked up at Harold and smiled with lots and lots of teeth.

"You swore on a dead cat," the voice repeated, only this time it was a perfect mockery of Joe.

Then, with a motion so quick Harold did not see it, the Fat Man grabbed him.

Bob the Dinosaur
Goes to Disneyland

. . . .

Another popcorn dream.

It's also inspired by the fact that my wife, Karen, and I had come back from Disneyland and I had a mouse ear hat, and for my birthday Karen had given me an inflatable dinosaur. I named it Bob. I ate popcorn, woke up the next morning with a dream about Bob in my mind, and this came out.

For Jeff Banks

For a birthday present, Fred's wife, Karen, bought him a plastic, inflatable dinosaur—a Tyrannosaurus Rex. It was in a cardboard box, and Fred thanked her and took the dinosaur downstairs to his study and took it out of the box and spent twenty minutes taking deep breaths and blowing air into it.

When the dinosaur was inflated, he sat it in front of his bookshelves, and as a joke, got a mouse ear hat he had bought at Disneyland three years before, and put it on the dinosaur's head and named it Bob.

Immediately, Bob wanted to go to Disneyland. There was no snuffing the ambition. He talked about it night and day, and it got so the study was no place to visit, because Bob would become most unpleasant on the matter. He scrounged around downstairs at night, pacing the floor, singing the Mouseketeer theme loud and long, waking up Fred and

Karen, and when Fred would come downstairs to reason with Bob, Bob wouldn't listen. He wouldn't have a minute's worth of it. No sir, he by golly wanted to go to Disneyland.

Fred said to Karen, "You should have bought me a Brontosaurus, or maybe a Stegosaurus. I have a feeling they'd have been easier to reason with."

Bob kept it up night and day. "Disneyland, Disneyland, I want to go to Disneyland. I want to see Mickey. I want to see Donald." It was like some kind of mantra, Bob said it so much. He even found some old brochures on Disneyland that Fred had stored in his closet, and Bob spread them out on the floor and lay down near them and studied the pictures and wagged his great tail and looked wistful.

"Disneyland," he would whisper. "I want to go to Disneyland."

And when he wasn't talking about it, he was mooning. He'd come up to breakfast and sit in two chairs at the table and stare blankly into the syrup on his pancakes, possibly visualizing the Matterhorn ride or Sleeping Beauty's castle. It got so it was a painful thing to see. And Bob got mean. He chased the neighbor's dogs and tore open garbage sacks and fought with the kids on the bus and argued with his teachers and took up slovenly habits, like throwing his used Kleenex on the floor of the study. There was no living with that dinosaur.

Finally, Fred had had enough, and one morning at breakfast, while Bob was staring into his pancakes, moving his fork through them lazily, but not really trying to eat them (and Fred had noticed that Bob had lost weight and looked as if he needed air), Fred said, "Bob, we've decided that you may go to Disneyland."

"What?" Bob said, jerking his head up so fast his mouse hat flew off and his fork scraped across his plate with a sound like a fingernail on a blackboard. "Really?"

"Yes, but you must wait until school is out for the summer, and you really have to act better."

"Oh, I will, I will," Bob said.

Well now, Bob was one happy dinosaur. He quit throwing Kleenex down and bothering the dogs and the kids on the bus and his teachers, and in fact, he became a model citizen. His school grades even picked up.

Finally, the big day came, and Fred and Karen bought Bob a suit of clothes and a nice John Deere cap, but Bob would have nothing to do with the new duds. He wore his mouse ear hat and a sweatshirt he had bought at Goodwill with a faded picture of Mickey Mouse on it with the word Disneyworld inscribed above it. He even insisted on carrying a battered Disney lunchbox he had picked up at the Salvation Army, but other than that, he was very cooperative.

Fred gave Bob plenty of money and Karen gave him some tips on how to eat a balanced meal daily, and then they drove him to the airport in the back of the pickup. Bob was so excited he could hardly sit still in the airport lounge, and when his seat section was called, he gave Fred and Karen quick kisses and pushed in front of an old lady and darted onto the plane.

As the plane lifted into the sky, heading for California and Disneyland, Karen said, "He's so happy. Do you think he'll be all right by himself?"

"He's very mature," Fred said. "He has his hotel arrangements, plenty of money, a snack in his lunchbox and lots of common sense. He'll be all right."

At the end of the week, when it was time for Bob to return, Fred and Karen were not available to pick him up at the airport. They made arrangements with their next-door neighbor, Sally, to do the job for them. When they got home, they could hear Bob playing the stereo in the study, and they went down to see him.

The music was loud and heavy metal and Bob had never listened to that sort of thing before. The room smelled of smoke, and not cigarettes. Bob was lying on the floor reading, and at first, Fred and Karen thought it was the Disney brochures, but then they saw those wadded up in the trashcan by the door.

Bob was looking at a girlie magazine and a reefer was hanging out of his mouth. Fred looked at Karen and Karen was clearly shaken.

"Bob?" Fred said.

"Yeah," Bob said without looking up from the foldout, and his tone was surly.

"Did you enjoy Disneyland?"

Bob carefully took the reefer out of his mouth and thumped ash on the carpet. There was the faintest impression of tears in his eyes. He stood up and tossed the reefer down and ground it into the carpet with his foot.

"Did . . . did you see Mickey Mouse?" Karen asked.

"Shit," Bob said, "there isn't any goddam mouse. It's just some guy in a suit. The same with the duck." And with that, Bob stalked into the bathroom and slammed the door and they couldn't get him out of there for the rest of the day.

On a Dark October

This is a favorite of mine. I like it because I could feel the transition from the type of story I had been writing—influenced by what Stan Wiater calls the California school of horror, meaning Bradbury, Matheson, Beaumont, Nolan, etc., over into the East Texas school of horror, members of this group being me and Ardath Mayhar, I guess.

I also liked it because it was simple and dark, and made, in a minor way, a statement or two that interested me. One of those statements was removed with a simple change by David Silva when it appeared in THE HORROR SHOW. He feared controversy. I couldn't see it, but I understood Dave's concern and complied, reluctantly, and when it was reprinted later in BEST OF THE HORROR SHOW, I requested it be changed back. It was. No controversy ensued, and I think most readers who read it now will wonder what the hell could have possibly been controversial.

For Dave Silva

The October night was dark and cool. The rain was thick. The moon was hidden behind dark clouds that occasionally flashed with lightning, and the sky rumbled as if it were a big belly that was hungry and needed filling.

A white Chrysler New Yorker came down the street and pulled up next to the curb. The driver killed the engine and the lights, turned to look at the building that sat on the block, an ugly tin thing with a weak light bulb shielded by a tin-hat shade over a fading sign that read BOB'S GA-RAGE. For a moment the driver sat unmoving, then he reached over, picked up the newspaper-wrapped package on the seat and put it in his lap. He opened it slowly. Inside was a shiny, oily, black-handled, ball peen hammer.

He lifted the hammer, touched the head of it to his free palm. It left a small smudge of grease there. He closed his hand, opened it, rubbed his fingers together. It felt just like . . . but he didn't want to think of that. It would all happen soon enough.

He put the hammer back in the papers, rewrapped it, wiped his fingers on the outside of the package. He pulled a raincoat from the back seat and put it across his lap. Then, with hands resting idly on the wheel, he sat silently.

A late model blue Ford pulled in front of him, left a space at the garage's drive, and parked. No one got out. The man in the Chrysler did not move.

Five minutes passed and another car, a late model Chevy, parked directly behind the Chrysler. Shortly thereafter three more cars arrived, all of them were late models. None of them blocked the drive. No one got out.

Another five minutes skulked by before a white van with MERTZ'S MEATS AND BUTCHER SHOP written on the side pulled around the Chrysler, then backed up the drive, almost to the garage door. A man wearing a hooded raincoat and carrying a package got out of the van, walked to the back and opened it.

The blue Ford's door opened, and a man dressed simi-larly, carrying a package under his arm, got out and went up the driveway. The two men nodded at one another. The man who had gotten out of the Ford unlocked the garage and slid the door back.

Car doors opened. Men dressed in raincoats, carrying

packages, got out and walked to the back of the van. A couple of them had flashlights and they flashed them in the back of the vehicle, gave the others a good view of what was there—a burlap wrapped, rope-bound bundle that wiggled and groaned.

The man who had been driving the van said, "Get it out."

Two of the men handed their packages to their comrades and climbed inside, picked up the squirming bundle, carried it into the garage. The others followed. The man from the Ford closed the door.

Except for the beams of the two flashlights, they stood close together in the darkness, like strands of flesh that had suddenly been pulled into a knot. The two with the bundle broke away from the others, and with their comrades directing their path with the beams of their flashlights, they carried the bundle to the grease rack and placed it between two wheel ramps. When that was finished, the two who had carried the bundle returned to join the others, to reform that tight knot of flesh.

Outside the rain was pounding the roof like tossed lug bolts. Lightning danced through the half-dozen small, barred windows. Wind shook the tin garage with a sound like a rattlesnake tail quivering for the strike, then passed on.

No one spoke for awhile. They just looked at the bundle. The bundle thrashed about and the moaning from it was louder than ever.

"All right," the man from the van said.

They removed their clothes, hung them on pegs on the wall, pulled their raincoats on.

The man who had been driving the blue Ford—after looking carefully into the darkness—went to the grease rack. There was a paper bag on one of the ramps. Earlier in the day he had placed it there himself. He opened it and took out a handful of candles and a book of matches. Using a match to guide him, he placed the candles down the length of the ramps, lighting them as he went. When he was finished, the garage glowed with a soft amber light. Except for the rear of the building. It was dark there.

The man with the candles stopped suddenly, a match flame wavering between his fingertips. The hackles on the back of his neck stood up. He could hear movement from the dark part of the garage. He shook the match out quickly and joined the others. Together, the group unwrapped their packages and gripped the contents firmly in their hands— hammers, brake-over handles, crowbars, heavy wrenches. Then all of them stood looking toward the back of the garage, where something heavy and sluggish moved.

The sound of the garage clock—a huge thing with DRINK COCA-COLA emblazoned on its face—was like the ticking of a time bomb. It was one minute to midnight.

Beneath the clock, visible from time to time when the glow of the candles was whipped that way by the draft, was a calendar. It read OCTOBER and had a picture of a smiling boy wearing overalls, standing amidst a field of pumpkins. The 31st was circled in red.

Eyes drifted to the bundle between the ramps now. It had stopped squirming. The sound it was making was not quite a moan. The man from the van nodded at one of the men, the one who had driven the Chrysler. The Chrysler man went to the bundle and worked the ropes loose, folded back the burlap. A frightened black youth, bound by leather straps and gagged with a sock and a bandana, looked up at him wide-eyed. The man from the Chrysler avoided looking back. The youth started squirming, grunting, and thrashing. Blood beaded around his wrists where the leather was tied, boiled out from around the loop fastened to his neck; when he kicked, it boiled faster because the strand had been drawn around his neck, behind his back and tied off at his ankles.

There came a sound from the rear of the garage again,

louder than before. It was followed by a sudden sigh that might have been the wind working its way between the rafters.

The van driver stepped forward, spoke loudly to the back of the garage. "We got something for you, hear me? Just like always we're doing our part. You do yours. I guess that's all I got to say. Things will be the same come next October. In your name, I reckon."

For a moment—just a moment—there was a glimmer of a shape when the candles caught a draft and wafted their bright heads in that direction. The man from the van stepped back quickly. "In your name," he repeated. He turned to the men. "Like always, now. Don't get the head until the very end. Make it last."

The faces of the men took on an expression of grimness, as if they were all playing a part in a theatric production and had been told to look that way. They hoisted their tools and moved toward the youth.

What they did took a long time.

When they finished, the thing that had been the young black man looked like a gigantic hunk of raw liver that had been chewed up and spat out. The raincoats of the men were covered in a spray of blood and brains. They were panting.

"Okay," said the man from the van.

They took off their raincoats, tossed them in a metal bin near the grease rack, wiped the blood from their hands, faces, ankles and feet with shop rags, tossed those in the bin and put on their clothes.

The van driver yelled to the back of the garage. "All yours. Keep the years good, huh?"

They went out of there and the man from the Ford locked the garage door. Tomorrow he would come to work as always. There would be no corpse to worry about, and a quick dose of gasoline and a match would take care of the contents in the bin. Rain ran down his back and made him shiver.

Each of the men went out to their cars without speaking. Tonight they would all go home to their young, attractive wives and tomorrow they would all go to their prosperous businesses and they would not think of this night again. Until next October.

They drove away. Lightning flashed. The wind howled. The rain beat the garage like a cat-o'-nine-tails. And inside there were loud sucking sounds punctuated by grunts of joy.

My Dead Dog, Bobby

This one came quickly and was written quickly. I sent it to THE HORROR SHOW and Dave Silva accepted it. It came out and surprised me by getting a lot of response. People at signings often mention it, and it has been Xeroxed and passed about by numerous people, recited even, and read over Welsh radio.

Go figure.

It was, by the way, inspired by eating too much popcorn and having bad dreams.

Contrary to what some might think, I love animals. Dogs especially.

For David Webb

My dead dog, Bobby, doesn't do tricks anymore. In fact, to look that sucker in the eye I either have to get down on my knees and put my head to the ground or prop him up with a stick.

I've thought of nailing his head to the shed out back, that way maybe the ants won't be so bad. But as my Old Man says, "Ants can climb." So, maybe that isn't such a good idea after all.

He was such a good dog, though, and I hate to see him rot away. But I'm also tired of carrying him around with me in a sack, lugging him into the freezer morning and night.

One thing, though. Getting killed broke him from chasing cars, which is how he got mashed in the first place. Now, to get him to play with cars, I have to go out to the edge of the Interstate and throw him and his sack at them, and when he gets caught under the tires and bounces up, I have to use my foot to push on one end of him to make the other end fill up with guts again. I get so I really kind of hate to look in the sack at the end of the day, and I have to admit giving him his goodnight kiss on the lips is not nearly as fun as it used to be. He has a smell and the teeth that have been smashed through his snout are sharp and stick out every which way and sometimes cut my face.

I'm going to take Bobby down to the lake again tomorrow. If you tie him to a blowed up inner-tube he floats. It's not a bad way to cool off from a hot day, and it also drowns the ants and maggots and such.

We kept my little brother in pretty good shape for six months that way. It wasn't until we started nailing him to the shed out back that he got to looking ragged. It wasn't the ants crawling up there and getting him, it was the damn nails. We ran out of good places to drive them after his ear came off, and we had to use longer and longer nails to put through his head and neck and the like. Pulling the nails out everyday with the hammer claw didn't do him any good either.

My Old Man said that if he had to do it over, he wouldn't have hit my brother so hard with that chair. But he said that about my little sister too when he kicked her head in. She didn't keep long, by the way. We didn't know as many tricks then as we do now.

Well, I hope I can get Bobby back in this sack. He's starting to swell and come apart on me. I'm sort of ready to get him packed away so I can get home and see Mom. I always look at her for a few minutes before I put Bobby in the freezer with her.

Bestsellers
Guaranteed

In 1983 I had the worst year of my life. Part of the reason was I started writing different types of stories: "The Pit" and "By Bizarre Hands" being examples, and none of it was selling. No one even knew what they were. Every anthology or magazine rejected them, or wanted me to put a twist in the end, which assured me they didn't have a clue what I was doing. I refused. So, I didn't sell. Things got worse. I decided to write a more traditional tale, but something that would contain the seeds of my frustration, and I suppose my reading a number of ill-written bestsellers added to that frustration, and this came out.

For Anibal Martinez

Larry had a headache, as he often did. It was those all-night stints at the typewriter, along with his job and his boss, Fraggerty, yelling for him to fry the burgers faster, to dole them out lickity-split on mustard-covered sesame seed buns.

Burgers and fries, typing paper and typewriter ribbons—the ribbons as gray and faded as the thirty-six years of his life. There really didn't seem to be any reason to keep on living. Another twenty to thirty years of this would be foolish. Then again, that seemed the only alternative. He was too cowardly to take his own life.

Washing his face in the bathroom sink, Larry jerked a

rough paper towel from the rack and dried off, looking at himself in the mirror. He was starting to look like all those hacks of writer mythology. The little guys who turned out the drek copy. The ones with the blue-veined, alcoholic noses and eyes like volcanic eruptions.

"My God," he thought, "I look forty easy. Maybe even forty-five."

"You gonna stay in the can all day?" a voice yelled through the door. It was Fraggerty, waiting to send him back to the grill and the burgers. The guy treated him like a bum.

A sly smile formed on Larry's face as he thought: "I am a bum. I've been through three marriages, sixteen jobs, eight typewriters, and all I've got to show for it are a dozen articles, all of them in obscure magazines that either paid in copies or pennies." He wasn't even as good as the hack he looked like. The hack could at least point to a substantial body of work, drek or not.

And I've been at this . . . God, twelve years! An article a year. Some average. Not even enough to pay back his typing supplies.

He thought of his friend Mooney—or James T. Mooney, as he was known to his fans. Yearly, he wrote a bestseller. It was a bestseller before it hit the stands. And except for Mooney's first novel, THE GOODBYE REEL, a detective thriller, all of them had been dismal. In fact, dismal was too kind a word. But the public lapped them up.

What had gone wrong with his own career? He used to help Mooney with his plots; in fact, he had helped him work out his problems on THE GOODBYE REEL, back when they had both been scrounging their livings and existing out of a suitcase. Then Mooney had moved to Houston, and a year later THE GOODBYE REEL had hit the stands like an atomic bomb. Made record sales in hardback and paper, and gathered in a movie deal that boggled the imagination.

Being honest with himself, Larry felt certain that he could

say he was a far better writer than Mooney. More commercial, even. So why had Mooney gathered the laurels while he bagged burgers and ended up in a dirty restroom contemplating the veins in his nose?

It was almost too much to bear. He would kill to have a bestseller. Just one. That's all he'd ask. Just one.

"Tear the damned crapper out of there and sit on it behind the grill!" Fraggerty called through the door. "But get out here. We got customers lined up down the block."

Larry doubted that, but he dried his hands, combed his hair and stepped outside.

Fraggerty was waiting for him. Fraggerty was a big fat man with bulldog jowls and perpetual blossoms of sweat beneath his meaty arms. Mid-summer, dead of winter—he had them.

"Hey," Fraggerty said, "you work here or what?"

"Not anymore," Larry said. "Pay me up."

"What?"

"You heard me, fat ass. Pay up!"

"Hey, don't get tough about it. All right. Glad to see you hike."

Five minutes later, Larry was leaving the burger joint, a fifty-dollar check in his pocket.

He said aloud: "Job number seventeen."

The brainstorm had struck him right when he came out of the restroom. He'd go see Mooney. He and Mooney had been great friends once, before all that money and a new way of living had carried Mooney back and forth to Houston and numerous jet spots around the country and overseas.

Maybe Mooney could give him a connection, an *in*, as it was called in the business. Before, he'd been too proud to ask, but now he didn't give a damn if he had to crawl and lick boots. He had to sell his books; had to let the world know he existed.

Without letting the landlord know, as he owed considerable back rent, he cleaned out his apartment.

Like his life, there was little there. A typewriter, copies of his twelve articles, a few clothes and odds and ends. There weren't even any books. He'd had to sell them all to pay his rent three months back.

In less than twenty minutes, he snuck out without being seen, loaded the typewriter and his two suitcases in the trunk of his battered Chevy, and looked up at the window of his dingy apartment. He lifted his middle finger in salute, climbed in the car and drove away.

Mooney was easy to find. His estate looked just the part for the residence of a bestselling author. A front lawn the size of a polo field, a fountain of marble out front, and a house that looked like a small English castle. All this near downtown Houston.

James T. Mooney looked the part, too. He answered the door in a maroon smoking jacket with matching pajamas. He had on a pair of glossy leather bedroom slippers that he could have worn with a suit and tie. His hair was well-groomed with just the right amount of gray at the temples. There was a bit of a strained look about his eyes, but other than that he was the picture of health and prosperity.

"Well, I'll be," Mooney said. "Larry Melford. Come in."

The interior of the house made the outside like a barn. There were paintings and sculptures and shelves of first edition books. On one wall, blown up to the size of movie posters and placed under glass and frame, were copies of the covers of his bestsellers. All twelve of them. A thirteenth glass and frame stood empty beside the others, waiting for the inevitable.

They chatted as they walked through the house, and Mooney said, "Let's drop off in the study. We can be comfortable there. I'll have the maid bring us some coffee or iced tea."

"I hope I'm not interrupting your writing," Larry said.

"No, not at all. I'm finished for the day. I usually just work a couple hours a day."

A couple hours a day? thought Larry. A serpent of envy crawled around in the pit of his stomach. For the last twelve years, he had worked a job all day and had written away most of the night, generally gathering no more than two to three hours' sleep a day. And here was Mooney writing these monstrous bestsellers and he only wrote a couple of hours in the mornings.

Mooney's study was about the size of Larry's abandoned apartment. And it looked a hell of a lot better. One side of the room was little more than a long desk covered with a word processor and a duplicating machine. The rest of the room was taken up by a leather couch and rows of bookshelves containing nothing but Mooney's work. Various editions of foreign publications, special collectors' editions, the leather-bound Christmas set, the paperbacks, the bound galleys of all the novels. Mooney was surrounded by his success.

"Sit down; take the couch," Mooney said, hauling around his desk chair. "Coffee or tea? I'll have the maid bring it."

"No, I'm fine."

"Well then, tell me about yourself."

Larry opened his mouth to start, and that's when it fell out. He just couldn't control himself. It was as if a dam had burst open and all the water of the world was flowing away. The anguish, the misery, the years of failure found expression.

When he had finished telling it all, his eyes were

glistening. He was both relieved and embarrassed. "So you see, Mooney, I'm just about over the edge. I'm craving success like an addict craves a fix. I'd kill for a bestseller."

Mooney's face seemed to go lopsided. "Watch that kind of talk."

"I mean it. I'm feeling so small right now, I'd have to look up to see a snake's belly. I'd lie, cheat, steal, kill—anything to get published in a big way. I don't want to die and leave nothing of me behind."

"And you don't want to miss out on the good things either, right?"

"Damned right. You've got it."

"Look, Larry, worry less about the good things and just write your books. Ease up some, but do it your own way. You may never have a big bestseller, but you're a good writer, and eventually you'll crack and be able to make a decent living."

"Easy for you to say, Mooney."

"In time, with a little patience . . ."

"I'm running out of time and patience. I'm emotionally drained, whipped. What I need is an *in*, Mooney, an *in*. A name. Anything that can give me a break."

"Talent is the name of the game, Larry, not an *in*," Mooney said very softly.

"Don't give me that garbage. I've got talent and you know it. I used to help you with the plots of your short stories. And your first novel—remember the things I worked out for you there? I mean, come on, Mooney. You've read my writing. It's good. Damned good! I need help. An *in* can't hurt me. It may not help me much, but it's got to give me a damn sight better chance than I have now."

Larry looked at Mooney's face. Something seemed to be moving there behind the eyes and taut lips. He looked sad, and quite a bit older than his age. Well, okay. So he was offended by being asked right out to help a fellow writer.

That was too bad. Larry just didn't have the pride and patience anymore to beat around the bush.

"An *in*, huh?" Mooney finally said.

"That's right."

"You sure you wouldn't rather do it your way?"

"I've been doing it my way for twelve years. I want a break, Mooney."

Mooney nodded solemnly. He went over to his desk and opened a drawer. He took out a small, white business card and brought it over to Larry.

It read:

BESTSELLERS GUARANTEED
Offices in New York, Texas, California
and
Overseas

The left-hand corner of the card had a drawing of an open book, and the right-hand corner had three phone numbers. One of them was a Houston number.

"I met a lady when I first moved here," Mooney said, "a big name author in the romance field. I sort of got this thing going with her . . . finally asked her for . . . an *in*. And she gave me this card. We don't see each other anymore, Larry. We stopped seeing each other the day she gave it to me."

Larry wasn't listening. "This an editor?"

"No."

"An agent?"

"No."

"Publisher, book packager?"

"None of those things and a little of all, and a lot more."

"I'm not sure . . ."

"You wanted your *in*, so there it is. You just call that

number. And Larry, do me a favor. Never come here again."

The first thing Larry did when he left Mooney's was find a telephone booth. He dialed the Houston number and a crisp female voice answered: "Bestsellers Guaranteed."

"Are you the one in charge?"

"No sir, just hold on and I'll put you through to someone who can help you."

Larry tapped his finger on the phone shelf till a smooth-as-well-water male voice said: "B.G. here. May I be of assistance?"

"Uh . . . yes, a friend of mine . . . a Mr. James T. Mooney—"

"Of course, Mr. Mooney."

"He suggested . . . he gave me a card. Well, I'm a writer. My name is Larry Melford. To be honest, I'm not exactly sure what Mooney had in mind for me. He just suggested I call you."

"All we need to know is that you were recommended by Mr. Mooney. Where are you now?"

Larry gave the address of the 7-Eleven phone booth.

"Why don't you wait there . . . oh, say . . . twenty minutes and we'll send a car to pick you up? That suit you?"

"Sure, but . . ."

"I'll have an agent explain it to you when he gets there, okay?"

"Yes, yes, that'll be fine."

Larry hung up and stepped outside to lean on the hood of his car. By golly, he thought, that Mooney does have connections, and now after all these years, my thirteenth year of trying, maybe, just maybe, I'm going to get connected, too.

He lit a cigarette and watched the August heat waves

bounce around the 7-Eleven lot, and twenty minutes later, a tan, six-door limousine pulled up next to his Chevy.

The man driving the limo wore a chauffeur's hat and outfit. He got out of the car and walked around to the tinted, far backseat window and tapped gently on the glass. The window slid down with a short whoosh. A man dressed in black with black hair, a black mustache, and thick-rimmed black shades, looked out at Larry. He said, "Mr. Melford?"

"Yes," Larry said.

"Would you like to go around to the other side? Herman will open the door for you."

After Larry had slid onto the seat and Herman had closed the door behind him, his eyes were drawn to the plush interior of the car. Encased in the seat in front of them was a phone, a television set and a couple of panels that folded out. Larry felt certain one of them would be a small bar. Air-conditioning hummed softly. The car was nice enough and large enough to live in.

He looked across the seat at the man in black, who was extending his hand. They shook. The man in black said, "Just call me James, Mr. Melford."

"Fine. This is about . . . writing? Mooney said he could give me a . . . connection. I mean, I have work, plenty of it. Four novels, a couple of dozen short stories, a novella—of course I know that length is a dog to sell, but . . ."

"None of that matters," James said.

"This *is* about writing?"

"This is about bestsellers, Mr. Melford. That is what you want, isn't it? To be a bestselling author?"

"More than anything."

"Then you're our man and we're your organization."

Herman had eased in behind the wheel. James leaned forward over the seat and said firmly, "Drive us around." Leaning back, James touched a button on the door panel and a thick glass rose out of the seat in front of them and clicked into place in a groove in the roof.

"Now," James said, "shall we talk?"

As they drove, James explained, "I'm the agent assigned to you, and it's up to me to see if I can convince you to join our little gallery. But, if you should sign on with us, we expect you to remain loyal. You must consider that we offer a service that is unique, unlike any offered anywhere. We can guarantee that you'll hit the bestseller list once a year, every year, as long as you're with us.

"Actually, Mr. Melford, we're not a real old organization, though I have a hard time remembering the exact year we were founded—it predated the Kennedy assassination by a year."

"That would be sixty-two," Larry said.

"Yes, yes, of course. I'm terrible at years. But it's only lately that we've come into our own. Consider the bad state of publishing right now, then consider the fact that our clients have each had a bestseller this year—and they will next year, no matter how bad publishing may falter. Our clients may be the only ones with books, but each of their books will be a bestseller, and their success will, as it does every year, save the industry."

"You're a packager?"

"No. We don't actually read the books, Mr. Melford, we just make sure they're bestsellers. You can write a book about the Earth being invaded by giant tree toads from the moon, if you like, and we will guarantee it will be a bestseller."

"My God, you are connected."

"You wouldn't believe the connections we have."

"And what does your organization get out of this? How much of a percentage?"

"We don't take a dime."

"What?"

"Not a dime. For our help, for our guarantee that your books will be bestsellers, we ask only one thing. A favor. One favor a year. A favor for each bestseller."

"What's the favor?"

"We'll come to that in a moment. But before we do, let me make sure you understand what we have to offer. I mean, if you were successful—and I mean no offense by this—then you wouldn't be talking to me now. You need help. We can offer help. You're in your mid-thirties, correct? Yes, I thought so. Not really old, but a bit late to start a new career plan. People do it, but it's certainly no piece of cake, now, is it?"

Larry found that he was nodding in agreement.

"So," James continued, "what we want to do is give you success. We're talking money in the millions of dollars, Mr. Melford. Fame. Respect. Most anything you'd want would be at your command. Exotic foods and wines? A snap of the fingers. Books? Cars? Women? A snap of the fingers. Anything your heart desires and it's yours."

"But I have to make a small, initial investment, right?"

"Ah, suspicious by nature, are you?"

"Wouldn't you be? My God, you're offering me the world."

"So I am. But no . . . no investment. Picture this, Mr. Melford. You might get lucky and sell the work, might even have a bestseller. But the slots are getting smaller and smaller for new writers. And one reason for that is that our writers, our clients, are filling those slots, Mr. Melford. If it's between your book and one of our clients', and yours is ten times better written, our client will still win out. Every time."

"What you're saying is, the fix is in?"

"A crude way of putting it, but rather accurate. Yes."

"What about talent, craftsmanship?"

"I wouldn't know about any of that. I sell success, not books."

"But it's the public that puts out its money for these books. They make or break an author. How can you know what they'll buy?"

"Our advertising system is the best in the world. We know how to reach the public and how to convince. We also use subliminals, Mr. Melford. We flash images on television programs, theater films; we hide them in the art of wine and cigarette ads. Little things below conscious perception, but images that lock tight to the subconscious mind. People who would not normally pick up a book will buy our bestsellers."

"Isn't that dishonest?"

"Who's to tell in this day and age what's right and wrong? It's relative, don't you think, Mr. Melford?"

Larry didn't say anything.

"Look. The public pictures writers as rich, all of them. They don't realize that the average full-time writer barely makes a living. Most of them are out there starving, and for what? Get on the winning side for a change, Mr. Melford. Otherwise, spend the rest of your life living in roach motels and living off the crumbs tossed you by the publishing world. And believe me, Mr. Melford, if you fail to join up with us, crumbs are all you'll get. If you're lucky."

The limousine had returned to the 7-Eleven parking lot. They were parked next to Larry's car.

"I suppose," James said, "we've come to that point that the bullfighters call 'the moment of truth.' You sign on with us and you'll be on Easy Street for the rest of your life."

"But we haven't talked terms."

"No, we haven't. It's at this point that I must ask you to either accept or turn down our offer, Mr. Melford. Once I've outlined the terms, you must be in full agreement with us."

"Accept before I hear what this favor you've talked about is?"

"That's correct. Bestseller or Bohemian, Mr. Melford. Which is it? Tell me right now. My time is valuable."

Larry paused only a moment. "Very well. Count me in. In for a penny, in for a pound. What's the favor?"

"Each year, you assassinate someone for us."

Larry dove for the door handle, but it wouldn't open. It had been locked electronically. James grabbed him by the wrist and held him tightly, so tightly Larry thought his bones would shatter.

"I wouldn't," James said. "After what I've told you, you step out of this car and they'll find you in a ditch this afternoon, obviously the victim of some hit-and-run driver."

"That's . . . that's murder."

"Yes, it is," James said. "Listen to me. You assassinate whomever we choose. We're not discriminating as far as sex, color, religion or politics goes. Anyone who gets in our way dies. Simple as that. You see, Mr. Melford, we are a big organization. Our goal is world domination. You, and all our clients, are little helpers toward that goal. Who is more respected than a bestselling author? Who is allowed in places where others would not be allowed? Who is revered by public figures and the general public alike? An author—a bestselling author."

"But . . . it's murder."

"There will be nothing personal in it. It'll just be your part of the contract. One assassination a year that we'll arrange."

"But if you're so connected . . . why do it this way? Why not just hire a hit man?"

"In a sense, I have."

"I'm not an assassin. I've never even fired a gun."

"The amateur is in many ways better than the professional. He doesn't fall into a pattern. When the time comes, we will show you what you have to do. If you decide to be with us, that is.''

''And if not?''

''I told you a moment ago. The ditch. The hit-and-run driver.''

Suddenly, Herman was standing at the door, his hand poised to open it.

''Which is it, Mr. Melford? I'm becoming impatient. A ditch or a bestseller? And if you have any ideas about going to the police, don't. We have friends there, and you might accidentally meet one. Now, your decision.''

''I'm in,'' Larry said, softly. ''I'm in.''

''Good,'' James said, taking Larry's hand. ''Welcome aboard. You get one of those books of yours out, pick out a publisher, and mail it in. And don't bother with return postage. We'll take care of the rest. Congratulations.''

James motioned to Herman. The door opened. Larry got out. And just before the door closed, James said, ''If you should have trouble coming up with something, getting something finished, just let me know and we'll see that it gets written for you.''

Larry stood on the sidewalk, nodding dumbly. Herman returned to the driver's seat, and a moment later the tan limo from Bestsellers Guaranteed whispered away.

James was as good as his word. Larry mailed off one of his shopworn novels, a thriller entitled TEXAS BACKLASH, and a contract for a half million dollars came back, almost by return mail.

Six months later, the book hit the bestseller list and rode there for a comfortable three months. It picked up a two-million-dollar paperback sale and a bigshot movie producer purchased it for twice that amount.

Larry now had a big mansion outside of Nacogdoches,

Texas, with a maid, a cook, two secretaries and a professional yard man. Any type of food he wanted was his for the asking. Once he had special seafood flown in from the East Coast to Houston and hauled from there to his door by refrigerated truck.

Any first edition book he wanted was now within his price range. He owned four cars, two motorcycles, a private airplane and a yacht.

He could own anything—even people. They hopped at his every word, his most casual suggestion. He had money, and people wanted to satisfy those with money. Who knows, maybe it would rub off on them.

And there were women. Beautiful women. There was even one he had grown to care for, and believed cared for him instead of his money and position. Lovely Luna Malone.

But in the midst of all this finery, there was the favor. The thought of it rested on the back of his mind like a waiting vulture. And when a year had gone by, the vulture swooped in.

On a hot August day, the tan limo from Bestsellers Guaranteed pulled up the long, scenic drive to Larry's mansion. A moment later, Larry and James were in Larry's study and Herman stood outside the closed door with his arms akimbo, doing what he did best. Waiting silently.

James was dressed in black again. He still wore the thick-framed sun shades. "You know what I've come for, don't you?"

Larry nodded. "The favor."

"On March fifteenth, Bestsellers Guaranteed will arrange for an autograph party in Austin for your new bestseller, whatever that may be. At eleven-fifteen, you will excuse yourself to go upstairs to the men's room. Next door to it is a janitor's lounge. It hasn't been used in years. It's locked but we will provide you with the key.

"At the rear of the lounge is a restroom. Lift off the back of the commode and you will discover eight small packages taped to the inside. Open these and fit them together and you'll have a very sophisticated air rifle. One of the packages will contain a canister of ice, and in the middle, dyed red, you will find a bullet-shaped projectile of ice. The air gun can send that projectile through three inches of steel without the ice shattering.

"You will load the gun, go to the window, and at exactly eleven-twenty-five, the Governor will drive by in an open car in the midst of the parade. A small hole has been cut in the restroom window. It will exactly accommodate the barrel of the rifle and the scope will fit snugly against the glass. You will take aim, and in a manner of seconds, your favor for this year will be done."

"Why the Governor?"

"That is our concern."

"I've never shot a rifle."

"We'll train you. You have until March. You won't need to know much more than how to put the rifle together and look through the scope. The weapon will do the rest."

"If I refuse?"

"The bestselling author of TEXAS BACKLASH will be found murdered in his home by a couple of burglars, and a couple of undesirables will be framed for the crime. Don't you think that has a nicer ring to it than the hit-and-run program I offered you before? Or perhaps, as a warning, we'll do something to your lady friend. What's her name . . . Luna?"

"You wouldn't!"

"If it would offer incentive or achieve our desired goals, Mr. Melford, we would do anything."

"You bastard!"

"That'll be quite enough, Mr. Melford. You've reaped the rewards of our services, and now we expect to be repaid.

It seems a small thing to ask for your success—and certainly you wouldn't want to die at the hands of other bestselling authors, the ones who will ultimately be your assassins.''

In spite of the air-conditioning, Larry had begun to sweat. "Just who are you guys, really?"

"I've told you. We're an organization with big plans. What we sponsor more than anything else, Mr. Melford, is moral corruption. We feed on those who thrive on greed and ego; put them in positions of power and influence. We belong to a group, to put it naively, who believe that once the silly concepts of morality and honor break down, then we, who really know how things work, can take control and make them work to our advantage. To put it even more simply, Mr. Melford. We will own it all.''

"I . . . I can't just cold-bloodedly murder someone."

"Oh, I think you can. I've got faith in you. Look around you, Mr. Melford. Look at all you've got. Think of what you've got to lose, then tell me if you can murder from a distance someone you don't even know. I'll wait outside with Herman for your answer. You have two minutes.''

From the March fifteenth edition of *The Austin Statesman,* a front-page headline: "GOVERNOR ASSASSINATED, ASSASSIN SOUGHT.''

From the same issue, page 4B: "BESTSELLING AUTHOR, LARRY MELFORD, SIGNS BOOKS.''

Six months later, in the master bedroom of Larry Melford's estate, Larry was sitting nude in front of the dresser mirror, clipping unruly nose hairs. On the bed behind him, nude, dark, luscious, lay Luna Malone. There was a healthy glow of sweat on her body as she lay with two pillows propped under her head; her raven hair was like an explosion of ink against their whiteness.

"Larry," she said, "you know, I've been thinking . . . I mean there's something I've been wanting to tell you, but haven't said anything about it because . . . well, I was afraid you might get the wrong idea. But now that we've known each other a while, and things look solid . . . Larry, I'm a writer."

Larry quit clipping his nose hairs. He put the clipper on the dresser and turned very slowly. "You're what?"

"I mean, I want to be. And not just now, not just this minute. I've always wanted to be. I didn't tell you, because I was afraid you'd laugh, or worse, think I'd only got to know you so you could give me an *in*, but I've been writing for years and have sent book after book, story after story in, and just know I'm good, and well . . ."

"You want me to look at it?"

"Yeah, but more than that, Larry. I need an *in*. It's what I've always wanted. To write a bestseller. I'd kill for . . ."

"Get out! Get the hell out!"

"Larry, I didn't meet you for that reason . . ."

"Get the hell out or I'll throw you out."

"Larry . . ."

"Now!" He stood up from the chair, grabbed her dressing gown. "Just go. Leave everything. I'll have it sent to you. Get dressed and never let me see you again."

"Aren't you being a little silly about this? I mean . . ."

Larry moved as fast as an eagle swooping down on a field mouse. He grabbed her shoulder and jerked her off the bed onto the floor.

"All right, you bastard, all right." Luna stood. She grabbed the robe and slipped into it. "So I did meet you for an *in;* what's wrong with that? I bet you had some help along the way. It sure couldn't have been because you're a great writer. I can hardly force myself through that garbage you write."

He slapped her across the cheek so hard she fell back on the bed.

Holding her face, she got up, gathered her clothes and walked stiffly to the bathroom. Less than a minute later, she came out dressed, the robe over her shoulder.

"I'm sorry about hitting you," Larry said. "But I meant what I said about never wanting to see you again."

"You're crazy, man. You know that? Crazy. All I asked you for was an *in*, just . . ."

Luna stopped talking. Larry had lifted his head to look at her. His eyes looked as dark and flat as the twin barrels of a shotgun.

"Don't bother having Francis drive me home. I'll call a cab from downstairs, Mr. Bigshot Writer."

She went out, slamming the bedroom door. Larry got up and turned off the light, went back to the dresser chair and sat in the darkness for a long time.

Nearly a year and a half later, not long after completing a favor for Bestsellers Guaranteed, and acquiring a somewhat rabid taste for alcoholic beverages, Larry was in the Houston airport waiting to catch a plane for Hawaii for a long vacation when he saw a woman in the distance who looked familiar. She turned and he recognized her immediately. It was Luna Malone. Still beautiful, a bit more worldly looking, and dressed to the hilt.

She saw him before he could dart away. She waved. He smiled. She came over and shook hands with him. "Larry, you aren't still mad, are you?"

"No, I'm not mad. Good to see you. You look great."

"Thanks."

"Where're you going?"

"Italy. Rome."

"Pope country," Larry said with a smile, but at his words, Luna jumped.

"Yes . . . Pope country."

The announcer called for the flight to Rome, Italy. Luna and Larry shook hands again and she went away.

To kill time, Larry went to the airport bookstores. He found he couldn't even look at the big cardboard display with his latest bestseller in it. He didn't like to look at bestsellers by anyone. But something did catch his eye. It was the cardboard display next to his. The book was called THE LITTLE STORM, and appeared to be one of those steamy romance novels. But what had caught his eye was the big, emblazoned name of the author—LUNA MALONE.

Larry felt like a python had uncoiled inside of him. He felt worse than he had ever felt in his life.

"Italy, Rome," she had said.

"Pope country," he had said, and she jumped.

Larry stumbled back against the rack of his book, and his clumsiness knocked it over. The books tumbled to the floor. One of them slid between his legs and when he looked down he saw that it had turned over to its back. There was his smiling face looking up at him. Larry Melford, big name author, bestseller, a man whose books found their way into the homes of millions of readers.

Suddenly, Hawaii was forgotten and Larry was running, running to the nearest pay phone. What had James said about moral corruption? "We feed on those who thrive on greed and ego . . . once silly concepts of morality and honor break down . . . we will own it all."

The nightmare had to end. Bestsellers Guaranteed had to be exposed. He would wash his hands with blood and moral corruption no more. He would turn himself in.

With trembling hand, he picked up the phone, put in his change, and dialed the police.

From today's *Houston Chronicle*, front page headline: "POPE ASSASSINATED."

From the same edition, the last page before the Want Ads, the last paragraph: "BESTSELLING AUTHOR MURDERED IN HOME." The story follows: "Police suspect the brutal murder of author Larry Melford occurred when he surprised burglars in the act. Thus far, police have been unable to . . ."

Dog, Cat, and Baby

When my son, Keith, was born, we had a dog and a cat. Both fine critters, but there was a certain jealousy in the air when we brought Keith home. Up until that time, the pets had ruled the roost. This made me nervous. I had heard horrible stories and read horrible newspaper accounts of babies being killed by jealous pets.

The pets and the baby were never left alone, no matter how innocent they seemed. Fear of what might happen if they were left alone fostered this story.

For John Maclay

Dog did not like Baby. For that matter, Dog did not like Cat. But Cat had claws—sharp claws.

Dog had always gotten attention. Pat on head. "Here, boy, here's a treat. Nice dog. Good dog. Shake hands. Speak! Sit. Nice dog."

Now there was Baby.

Cat had not been problem, really.

Cat was liked, not loved by family. They petted Cat sometimes. Fed her. Did not mistreat her. But they not love her. Not way they loved Dog—before Baby.

Damn little pink thing that cried.

Baby got "Oooohs and Ahhs." When Dog tried to get close to Masters, they say, "Get back, boy. Not *now*."

When would be *now?*

Dog never see now. Always Baby get now. Dog get nothing. Sometimes they so busy with Baby it be all day before Dog get fed. Dog never get treats anymore. Could not remember last pat on head or "Good Dog!"

Bad business. Dog not like it.

Dog decide to do something about it.

Kill Baby. Then there be Dog, Cat again. They not love Cat, so things be okay.

Dog thought that over. Wouldn't take much to rip little Baby apart. Baby soft, pink. Would bleed easy.

Baby often put in Jumper which hung between doorway when Master Lady hung wash. Baby be easy to get then.

So Dog waited.

One day Baby put in Jumper and Master Lady go outside to hang wash. Dog looks at pink thing jumping, thinks about ripping to pieces. Thinks on it long and hard. Thought makes him so happy his mouth drips water. Dog starts toward Baby, making fine moment last.

Baby looks up, sees Dog coming toward it slowly, almost creeping. Baby starts to cry.

But before Dog can reach Baby, Cat jumps.

Cat been hiding behind couch.

Cat goes after Dog, tears Dog's face with teeth, with claws. Dog bleeds, tries to run. Cat goes after him.

Dog turns to bite.

Cat hangs claw in Dog's eye.

Dog yelps, runs.

Cat jumps on Dog's back, biting on top of head.

Dog tries to turn corner into bedroom. Cat, tearing at him with claws, biting with teeth, makes Dog lose balance. Dog running very fast, fast as he can go, hits the edge of doorway, stumbles back, falls over.

Cat gets off Dog.

Dog lies still.

Dog, Cat, and Baby 91

Dog not breathing.

Cat knows Dog is dead. Cat licks blood from claws, from teeth with rough tongue.

Cat has gotten rid of Dog.

Cat turns to look down hall where Baby is screaming.

Now for *other* one.

Cat begins to creep down hall.

The Shaggy House

Another story inspired by THE NIGHTRUNNERS.

In the book there's a scene where one of my characters sees the house where he is soon to live for the first time, and I gave a sort of over the top description of it that I thought worked quite well in context, but there was something in that description that spurred me to consider the house from another angle, a less grim one. What came out was this short story. It's a gonzo hoot with an echo of Bradbury and a lot of tongue in cheek.

My title was "Something Lumber This Way Comes," which my friend Bill Nolan, to put it mildly, hated. He suggested this title. Since I used the other title on a variation of this story which became a children's book, as yet unpublished, I agreed. Secretly, I still prefer the original title, and when and if it ever appears on the children's book, I'll be a happy man.

For William F. Nolan

The old Ford moved silently through the night, cruised down the street slowly. The driver, an elderly white-haired man, had his window down and he was paying more attention to looking out of it, studying the houses, than he was to his driving. The car bumped the curb. The old man cursed softly, whipped it back into the dark, silent street.

Beaumont Street came to a dead end. The old man turned around, drove back up. This was his third trip tonight, up and down the short street, and for the third time he was certain. The houses on Beaumont Street were dying, turning gray, growing ugly, looking dreadfully sick, and it all seemed to have happened overnight.

His own house was the sickest looking among them. The paint was peeling—he'd just had it painted last year!—the window panes looked like the bottom of a lover's leap for flies—yet there were no fly bodies—and there was a general sagginess about the place, as if it were old like himself and the spirit had gone out of its lumber bones.

The other houses on the block were not much better. A certain degree of that was to be expected. The houses were old, and the inhabitants of the houses, in many cases, were older. The entire block consisted of retired couples and singles, the youngest of which was a man in his late sixties. But still, the block had always taken pride in their houses, managed somehow to mow the lawns and get the painting done, and then one day it all goes to rot.

And it had happened the moment that creepy house had appeared in the neighborhood, had literally sprung up overnight on the vacant lot across from his house. A gothic-hideous house, as brown and dead looking as the late Fall grass.

Craziest thing, however, was the fact that no one had seen or heard it being built. Just one day the block had gone to bed and the next morning they had awakened to find the nasty old thing sitting over there, crouched like a big, hungry toad, the two upper story windows looking like cold, calculating eyes.

Who the hell ever heard of putting up a house overnight? For that matter, who ever heard of prefab, weathered gothics? And last, but not least, why had they not seen anyone come out of or go into the house? It had been there a week, and so far no one had moved in, and there were no rent ads in the paper for it. He had checked.

Of course, a certain amount of the mystery might be explained if his wife were correct.

"Why you old fool, they moved that house in there. And for that matter, Harry, they just might have moved it in while we were sitting on the front porch watching. We're so old we don't notice what goes on anymore."

Harry gnashed his false teeth together so hard he ground powder out of the bicuspids. "Well," he said to the interior of the car, "you may be old, Edith, but I'm not."

No, he wasn't so old that he hadn't noticed the change in the neighborhood, the way the houses seemed to be infected with that old ruin's disease. And he knew that old house was somehow responsible for the damage, and he intended to get to the bottom of it.

A shape loomed in the headlights. Harry slammed his foot on the brakes and screeched the tires sharply.

An elderly, balding man ambled around to Harry's side of the car and stuck his face through the open window.

"Lem!" Harry said. "You trying to commit suicide?"

"No, I was fixing to go over there and burn that damned house down."

"You too, Lem?"

"Me too. Saw you cruising around looking. Figured you'd figured what I'd figured."

Harry looked at Lem cautiously. "And what have we figured?"

"That damned old house isn't up to any good, and that something's got to be done about it before the whole neighborhood turns to ruins."

"You've noticed how the houses look?"

"Any fool with eyes in his head and a pair of glasses can see what's going on."

"But why?"

"Who gives a damn why, let's just do something. I got some matches here, and a can of lighter fluid in my coat pocket—"

"Lem, we can't just commit arson. Look, get in. I don't like sitting here in the street."

Lem turned to look at the house. They were almost even with it. "Neither do I. That thing gives me the creeps."

Lem went around and got in. Harry drove up the block, parked at the far end where the street intersected another. Lem got out his pipe and packed it, filled the Ford with the smell of cinnamon.

"You're gonna get cancer yet," Harry said.

"Being as I'm ninety, it'll have to work fast."

Harry gnashed his bicuspids again. There was a certain logic in that, and just a month ago Edith had talked him into giving up his cigars for health reasons.

After a moment Lem produced a flask from his coat pocket, unscrewed the lid and removed the pipe from his mouth. "Cheers."

Harry sniffed. "Is that whiskey?"

"Prune juice." Lem smiled slyly.

"I bet."

Lem tossed a shot down his throat. "Wheee," he said, lifting the bottle away from his face. "That'll put lead in your pencil!"

"Let me have a snort of that."

Harry drank, gave the flask back to Lem who capped it, returned it to his pocket and put his pipe back into his face.

Unconsciously, they had both turned in their seats to look out the back window of the Ford, so they could see the house. Harry thought that the high-peaked roof looked a lot like a witch's hat there in the moonlight.

"Bright night," Lem said. "Holy Christ, Harry."

"I see it, I see it."

The old house trembled, moved.

It turned its head. No other image could possibly come to mind. The house was flexible, and now its two upstairs windows were no longer facing across the street, they were looking down the street, toward Harry and Lem. Then the head turned again, looked in the other direction, like a cautious pedestrian about to step out into a traffic zone. The turning of its head sounded like the creaking of an old tree in a high wind.

"God," Harry said.

The house stood, revealed thick, peasant girl legs and feet beneath its firm, wooden skirt, and then it stepped from the lot and began crossing the street. As it went, a window on either side of the house went up, and two spindly arms appeared as if suddenly poked through short shirt sleeves. The arms and hands were not as thick as the legs and feet; the hands were nearly flat, the fingers like gnarled oak branches.

"It's heading for my house," Harry said.

"Shut up!" Lem said. "You're talking too loud."

"Edith!"

"Edith's all right," Lem said. "Betcha a dog to a doughnut it's the house it wants. Watch!"

The house's rubbery front porch lips curled back and the front door opened to reveal rows of long, hollow, wood-screw teeth. With a creak it bent to nestle its mouth against the apex of Harry's roof, to latch its teeth there like a leech attaching itself to a swimmer's leg. And then came the low, soft sucking sounds, like gentle winds moaning against your roof at night; a sound you hear in your dreams and you almost wake, but from the back of your head comes a little hypnotic voice saying: "Sleep. It's only the wind crying, touching your roof, passing on," and so you sleep.

A shingle fell from Harry's house, caught a breeze and glided into the street. The front porch sagged ever so slightly. There was the soft sound of snapping wood from somewhere deep within. The windows grew darker and the glass rattled frightened in its frames.

After what seemed an eternity, but could only have been moments, the thing lifted its grotesque head and something dark and fluid dripped from its mouth, dribbled down the roof of Harry's house and splashed in the yard. Then there was a sound from the gothic beast, a sound like a rattlesnake clacking, a sort of contented laughter from deep in its chest.

The house turned on its silly feet, crept and creaked, arms swinging, back across the street, turned to face Harry's house, then like a tired man home from work, it settled sighing into its place once more. The two upper story windows grew dark, as if thick lids had closed over them. The front porch lips smacked once, then there was silence and no movement.

Harry turned to Lem, who had replaced the pipe with the whiskey flask. The whiskey gurgled loudly in the cool Fall night.

"Did you see . . . ?"

"Of course I did," Lem said, lowering the flask, wiping a sleeve across his mouth.

"Can't be."

"Somehow it is."

"But how?"

Lem shook his head. "Maybe it's like those science fiction books I read, like something out of them, an alien, or worse yet, something that has always been among us but has gone undetected for the most part.

"Say it's some kind of great space beast that landed here on Earth, a kind of chameleon that can camouflage itself by looking like a house. Perhaps it's some kind of vampire. Only it isn't blood it wants, but the energy out of houses." Lem tipped up his flask again.

"Houses haven't got energy."

Lem lowered the flask. "They've got their own special

kind of energy. Listen: houses are built for the most part—least these houses were—by people who love them, people who wanted good solid homes. They were built before those soulless glass and plastic turd mounds that dot the skyline, before contractors were throwing dirt into the foundation instead of gravel, before they were pocketing the money that should have gone on good studs, two-by-fours and two-by-sixes. And these houses, the ones built with hope and love, absorbed these sensations, and what is hope and love but a kind of energy? You with me, Harry?

"I guess, but . . . oh, rave on."

"So the walls of these houses took in that love and held it, and maybe that love, that energy, became the pulse, the heartbeat of the house. See what I'm getting at, Harry?

"Who appreciates and loves their homes more than folks our age, people who were alive when folks cared about what they built, people, who in their old age, find themselves more home-ridden, more dependent upon those four walls, more grateful of anything that keeps out the craziness of this newer world, keeps out the wind and the rain and the sun and those who would do us harm?

"This thing, maybe it can smell out, sense the houses that hold the most energy, and along it comes in the dead of night and it settles in and starts to draw the life out of them, like a vampire sucking out a victim's blood, and where the vampire's victims get weak and sag and grow pale, our houses do much the same. Because, you see, Harry, they have become living things. Not living in the way we normally think of it, but in a sort of silent, watchful way."

Harry blinked several times. "But why did it take the form of a gothic type house, why not a simple frame?"

"Maybe the last houses it was among looked a lot like that, and when it finished it came here. And to it these houses look basically the same as all the others. You see,

Harry, it's not impersonating *our* houses, it's impersonating *a* house."

"That's wild, Lem."

"And the more I drink from this flask, the wilder I'll get. Take this for instance: it could look like anything. Consider all the ghettos in the world, the slums, the places that no amount of Federal Aid, money and repair seem to fix. Perhaps these chameleons, or whatever you want to call them, live there as well—because despair fills walls as much as love—and they become the top floors of rundown tenement houses, the shanties alongside other shanties on Louisiana rivers—"

"And they feed on this love or despair, this energy?"

"Exactly, and when it's sucked out, the houses die and the creatures move on."

"What are we going to do about it?"

Lem turned up the flask and swigged. When he lowered it, he said, "*Something*, that's for sure."

They left the car, cat-pawed across the street, crept through backyards toward the sleeping house. When they were almost to the lot where the house squatted, they stopped beneath a sycamore tree and wore its shadow. They passed the flask back and forth.

Way out beyond the suburbs, in the brain of the city, they could hear traffic sounds. And much closer, from the ship channel, came the forlorn hoot of a plodding tug.

"Now what?" Harry asked.

"We sneak up on it from the rear, around by the back door—"

"Back door! If the front door is its mouth, Lem, the back door must be its—"

"We're not going inside, we're going to snoop, stupid, then we're going to do something."

"Like what?"

"We'll cross that blazing tightwire when we get to it. Now move!"

They moved, came to the back door. Lem reached out to touch the doorknob. "How about this?" he whispered. "No knob, just a black spot that looks like one. From a distance—hell, up close—you couldn't tell it was a fake without touching. Come on, let's look in the windows."

"Windows?" Harry said, but Lem had already moved around the edge of the house, and when Harry caught up with him, he was stooping at one of the windows, looking in.

"This is crazy," Lem said. "There's a stairway and furniture and cobwebs even . . . No, wait a minute. Feel!"

Harry crept up beside him, reluctantly touched the window. It was most certainly not glass, and it was not transparent either. It was cold and hard like the scale of a fish.

"It's just an illusion, like the doorknob," Harry said.

"Only a more complicated type of illusion, something it does with its mind probably. There's no furniture, no stairs, no nothing inside there but some kind of guts, I guess, the juice of our houses."

The house shivered, sent vibrations up Harry's palm. Harry remembered those long arms that had come out of the side windows earlier. He envisioned one popping out now, plucking him up.

The house burped, loudly.

Suddenly Lem was wearing Harry for a hat.

"Get down off me," Lem said, "or you're going to wake up with a tube up your nose."

Harry climbed down. "It's too much for us, Lem. In the movies they'd bring in the army, use nukes."

Lem took the can of lighter fluid out of his coat pocket. It was the large economy size.

"Sssssshhhh," Lem said. He brought out his pocket knife and a book of matches.

"You're going to blow us up!"

Lem tore the lining out of one of his coat pockets, squirted lighter fluid on it, poked one end of the lining into the fluid can with the point of his knife. He put the rag-stuffed can on the ground, the matches beside it. Then he took his knife, stuck it quickly into the house's side, ripped down.

Something black and odorous oozed out. The house trembled.

"That's like a mosquito bite to this thing," Lem said. "Give me that can and matches."

"I don't like this," Harry said, but he handed the can and matches to Lem. Lem stuck the can halfway into the wound, let the rag dangle.

"Now run like hell," Lem said, and struck a match.

Harry started running toward the street as fast as his arthritic legs would carry him.

Lem lit the pocket lining. The fluid-soaked cloth jumped to bright life.

Lem turned to run. He hadn't gone three steps when the can blew. The heat slapped his back and the explosion thundered inside his head. He reached the street, looked back.

The house opened its front door and howled like a sixty-mile-an-hour tornado. The upstairs front window shades went up, eyes glinted savagely in the moonlight. A spear of flame spurted out of the house's side.

Harry was crossing the street, running for his house when he looked back. The creature howled again. Arms came out of its sides. All around windows went up and wings sprouted out of them.

"Jesus," Harry said, and he turned away from his house

so as not to lead it to Edith. He started up the street toward his car.

Lem came up behind him laughing. "Ha! Ha! Flame on!"

Harry glanced back.

The explosion had ignited internal gases and the thing was howling flames now. Its tongue flapped out and slapped the street. Its wings fluttered and it rose up into the sky.

Doors opened all down the block.

Windows went up.

Edith's head poked out of one of the windows. "Harry?"

"Be back, be back, be back," Harry said, and ran on.

Behind him Lem said, "Pacemaker, don't fail me now."

They reached the car wheezing.

"There . . . she . . . goes," Lem panted. "After it!"

A bright orange-red mass darted shrieking across the night sky, moved toward the ship channel, losing altitude.

The Ford coughed to life, hit the street. They went left, driving fast. Lem hung out of the window, pointing up, saying, "There it goes! Turn left. No, now over there. Turn right!"

"The ship channel!" Harry yelled. "It's almost to the ship channel."

"Falling, falling," Lem said.

It was.

They drove up the ship channel bridge. The house-thing blazed above them, moaned loud enough to shake the windows in the Ford. The sky was full of smoke.

Harry pulled over to the bridge railing, parked, jumped out with Lem. Other cars had pulled over. Women, men and children burst out of them, ran to the railing, looked and pointed up.

The great flaming beast howled once more, loudly, then fell, hit the water with a thunderous splash.

"Ah, ha!" Harry yelled. "Dammit, Lem, we've done it,

the block is free. Tomorrow we break out the paint, buy new windows, get some shingles . . .''

The last of the thing slipped under the waves with a hiss. A black cloud hung over the water for a moment, thinned to gray. There was a brief glow beneath the expanding ripples, then darkness.

Lem lifted his flask in toast. "Ha! Ha! Flame out!"

By the Hair
of the Head

. . . .

When I wrote this one, Charlie Grant's SHADOW anthologies were the only real game in town, and I wanted to gear a story in that direction for the simple reason that I wanted a check and I wanted to see if I could handle that type of story—quiet and casual, the cold hand at the back of the neck.

I had been rereading Arthur Machen, M. R. James, E. F. Benson, a lot of English writers I've read all my life, as well as numerous Alfred Hitchcock anthologies, and I thought it would be nice to see if I could capture the tone of those English masters, and the sort of stories one associates with Alfred Hitchcock in the anthologies that bear his name, and of course the now defunct, and much missed, television show, ALFRED HITCHCOCK PRESENTS.

This came out. Charlie made a few suggestions on the dialogue of Machen (told you I was reading Machen), which I had overdone in a sort of Scottish lilt that was about as accurate as Richard Nixon's memory of his presidency, and when I made those corrections, Charlie bought it and the story appeared in SHADOWS 6.

No one noticed. And it's easy to see why. That volume was filled with good stories by Steve Rasnic Tem, Jesse Osburn (a marvelous story; whatever happened to this guy?), Al Sarrantonio, Leigh Kennedy, and David Morrell.

For Charlie Grant

The lighthouse was gray and brutally weathered, kissed each morning by a cold, salt spray. Perched there among the rocks and sand, it seemed a last, weak sentinel against an encroaching sea; a relentless, pounding surf that had slowly swallowed up the shoreline and deposited it in the all-consuming belly of the ocean.

Once the lighthouse had been bright-colored, candy-striped like a barber's pole, with a high beacon light and a horn that honked out to the ships on the sea. No more. The lighthouse director, the last of a long line of sea watchers, had cashed in the job ten years back when the need died, but the lighthouse was now his and he lived there alone, bunked down nightly to the tune of the wind and the raging sea.

Below he had renovated the bottom of the tower and built rooms, and one of these he had locked away from all persons, from all eyes but his own.

I came there fresh from college to write my novel, dreams of being the new Norman Mailer dancing in my head. I rented in with him, as he needed a boarder to help him pay for the place, for he no longer worked and his pension was as meager as stale bread.

High up in the top was where we lived, a bamboo partition drawn between our cots each night, giving us some semblance of privacy, and dark curtains were pulled round the thick, foggy windows that traveled the tower completely around.

By day the curtains were drawn and the partition was pulled and I sat at my typewriter, and he, Howard Machen, sat with his book and his pipe, swelled the room full of gray smoke the thickness of his beard. Sometimes he rose and went below, but he was always quiet and never disturbed my work.

It was a pleasant life. Agreeable to both of us. Mornings we had coffee outside on the little railed walkway and had a word or two as well, then I went to my work and he to his book, and at dinner we had food and talk and brandies; sometimes one, sometimes two, depending on mood and the content of our chatter.

We sometimes spoke of the lighthouse and he told me of the old days, of how he had shone that light out many times on the sea. Out like a great, bright fishing line to snag the ships and guide them in; let them follow the light in the manner that Theseus followed Ariadne's thread.

"Was fine," he'd say. "That pretty old light flashing out there. Best job I had in all my born days. Just couldn't leave her when she shut down, so I bought her."

"It is beautiful up here, but lonely at times."

"I have my company."

I took that as a compliment, and we tossed off another brandy. Any idea of my writing later I cast aside. I had done four good pages and was content to spit the rest of the day away in talk and dreams.

"You say this was your best job," I said as a way of conversation. "What did you do before this?"

He lifted his head and looked at me over the briar and its smoke. His eyes squinted against the tinge of the tobacco. "A good many things. I was born in Wales. Moved to Ireland with my family, was brought up there, and went to work there. Learned the carpentry trade from my father. Later I was a tailor. I've also been a mason—note the rooms I built below with my own two hands—and I've been a boat builder and a ventriloquist in a magician's show."

"A ventriloquist?"

"Correct," he said, and his voice danced around me and seemed not to come from where he sat.

"Hey, that's good."

"Not so good really. I was never good, just sort of fell into it. I'm worse now. No practice, but I've no urge to take it up again."

"I've an interest in such things."

"Have you now?"

"Yes."

"Ever tried a bit of voice throwing?"

"No. But it interests me. The magic stuff interests me more. You said you worked in a magician's show?"

"That I did. I was the lead-up act."

"Learn any of the magic tricks, being an insider and all?"

"That I did, but that's not something I'm interested in," he said flatly.

"Was the magician you worked for good?"

"Damn good, m'boy. But his wife was better."

"His wife?"

"Marilyn was her name. A beautiful woman." He winked at me. "Claimed to be a witch."

"You don't say?"

"I do, I do. Said her father was a witch and she learned it and inherited it from him."

"Her father?"

"That's right. Not just women can be witches. Men too."

We poured ourselves another and exchanged sloppy grins, hooked elbows, and tossed it down.

"And another to meet the first," the old man said and poured. Then: "Here's to company." We tossed it off.

"She taught me the ventriloquism, you know," the old man said, relighting his pipe.

"Marilyn?"

"Right, Marilyn."

"She seems to have been a rather all-around lady."

"She was at that. And pretty as an Irish morning."

"I thought witches were all old crones, or young crones. Hook noses, warts . . ."

"Not Marilyn. She was a fine-looking woman. Fine bones, agate eyes that clouded in mystery, and hair the color of a fresh-robbed hive."

"Odd she didn't do the magic herself. I mean, if she was the better magician, why was her husband the star attraction?"

"Oh, but she did do magic. Or rather she helped McDonald to look better than he was, and he was some good. But Marilyn was better.

"Those days were different, m'boy. Women weren't the ones to take the initiative, least not openly. Kept to themselves. Was a sad thing. Back then it wasn't thought fittin' for a woman to be about such business. Wasn't ladylike. Oh, she could get sawed in half, or disappear in a wooden crate, priss and look pretty, but take the lead? Not on your life!"

I fumbled myself another brandy. "A pretty witch, huh?"

"Ummmm."

"Had the old pointed hat and broom passed down, so to speak?" My voice was becoming slightly slurred.

"It's not a laughin' matter, m'boy." Machen clenched the pipe in his teeth.

"I've touched a nerve, have I not? I apologize. Too much sauce."

Machen smiled. "Not at all. It's a silly thing, you're right. To hell with it."

"No, no, I'm the one who spoiled the fun. You were telling me she claimed to be the descendant of a long line of witches."

Machen smiled. It did not remind me of other smiles he had worn. This one seemed to come from a borrowed collection.

"Just some silly tattle is all. Don't really know much about it, just worked for her, m'boy." That was the end of that. Standing, he knocked out his pipe on the concrete floor and went to his cot.

For a moment I sat there, the last breath of Machen's pipe still in the air, the brandy still warm in my throat and stomach. I looked at the windows that surrounded the lighthouse, and everywhere I looked was my own ghostly reflection. It was like looking out through the compound eyes of an insect, seeing a multiple image.

I turned out the lights, pulled the curtains and drew the partition between our beds, wrapped myself in my blanket, and soon washed up on the distant shore of a recurring dream. A dream not quite in grasp, but heard like the far, fuzzy cry of a gull out from land.

It had been with me almost since moving into the tower. Sounds, voices . . .

A clunking noise like peg legs on stone . . .

. . . a voice, fading in, fading out . . . Machen's voice, the words not quite clear, but soft and coaxing . . . then solid and firm: "Then be a beast. Have your own way. Look away from me with your mother's eyes."

". . . your fault," came a child's voice, followed by other words that were chopped out by the howl of the sea wind, the roar of the waves.

". . . getting too loud. He'll hear . . ." came Machen's voice.

"Don't care . . . I . . ." lost voices now.

I tried to stir, but then the tube of sleep, nourished by the brandy, came unclogged, and I descended down into richer blackness.

Was a bright morning full of sun, and no fog for a change. Cool clear out there on the landing, and the sea even seemed to roll in soft and bounce against the rocks and lighthouse like puffy cotton balls blown on the wind.

I was out there with my morning coffee, holding the cup in one nand and grasping the railing with the other. It was a narrow area but safe enough, provided you didn't lean too far out or run along the walk when it was slick with rain. Machen told me of a man who had done just that and found himself plummeting over to be shattered like a dropped melon on the rocks below.

Machen came out with a cup of coffee in one hand, his unlit pipe in the other. He looked haggard this morning, as if a bit of old age had crept upon him in the night, fastened a straw to his face, and sucked out part of his substance.

"Morning," I said.

"Morning." He emptied his cup in one long draft. He balanced the cup on the metal railing and began to pack his pipe.

"Sleep bad?" I asked.

He looked at me, then at his pipe, finished his packing, and put the pouch away in his coat pocket. He took a long match from the same pocket, gave it fire with his thumbnail, lit the pipe. He puffed quite awhile before he answered me. "Not too well. Not too well."

"We drank too much."

"We did at that."

I sipped my coffee and looked at the sky, watched a snowy gull dive down and peck at the foam, rise up with a wriggling fish in its beak. It climbed high in the sky, became a speck of froth on the crystal blue.

"I had funny dreams," I said. "I think I've had them all along, since I came here. But last night they were stronger than ever."

"Oh?"

"Thought I heard your voice speaking to someone. Thought I heard steps on the stairs, or more like the plunking of peg legs, like those old sea captains have."

"You don't say?"

"And another voice, a child's."

"That right? Well . . . maybe you did hear me speakin'. I wasn't entirely straight with you last night. I do have quite an interest in the voice throwing, and I practice it from time to time on my dummy. Last night must have been louder than usual, being drunk and all.''

"Dummy?"

"My old dummy from the act. Keep it in the room below."

"Could I see it?"

He grimaced. "Maybe another time. It's kind of a private thing with me. Only bring her out when we're alone."

"Her?"

"Right. Name's Caroline, a right smart-looking girl dummy, rosy cheeked with blonde pigtails."

"Well, maybe someday I can look at her."

"Maybe someday." He stood up, popped the contents of the pipe out over the railing, and started inside. Then he turned: "I talk too much. Pay no mind to an old, crazy man."

Then he was gone, and I was there with a hot cup of coffee, a bright, warm day, and an odd, unexplained chill at the base of my bones.

Two days later we got on witches again, and I guess it was my fault. We hit the brandy hard that night. I had sold a short story for a goodly sum—my largest check to date—and we were celebrating and talking and saying how my fame would be as high as the stars. We got pretty sicky there, and to hear Machen tell it, and to hear me agree—no matter he hadn't read the story—I was another Hemingway, Wolfe, and Fitzgerald all balled into one.

"If Marilyn were here," I said thoughtlessly, drunk, "why we could get her to consult her crystal and tell us my literary future."

"Why that's nonsense, she used no crystal."

"No crystal, broom, or pointed hat? No eerie evil deeds for her? A white magician no doubt?"

"Magic is magic, m'boy. And even good intentions can backfire."

"Whatever happened to her, Marilyn I mean?"

"Dead."

"Old age?"

"Died young and beautiful, m'boy. Grief killed her."

"I see," I said, as you'll do to show attentiveness.

Suddenly, it was as if the memories were a balloon overloaded with air, about to burst if pressure were not taken off. So, he let loose the pressure and began to talk.

"She took her a lover, Marilyn did. Taught him many a thing, about love, magic, what have you. Lost her husband on account of it, the magician, I mean. Lost respect for herself in time.

"You see, there was this little girl she had, by her lover. A fine-looking sprite, lived until she was three. Had no proper father. He had taken to the sea and had never much entertained the idea of marryin' Marilyn. Keep them stringing was his motto then, damn his eyes. So he left them to fend for themselves."

"What happened to the child?"

"She died. Some childhood disease."

"That's sad," I said, "a little girl gone and having only sipped at life."

"Gone? Oh, no. There's the soul, you know."

I wasn't much of a believer in the soul and I said so.

"Oh, but there is a soul. The body perishes but the soul lives on."

"I've seen no evidence of it."

"But I have," Machen said solemnly. "Marilyn was determined that the girl would live on, if not in her own form, then in another."

"Hogwash!"

Machen looked at me sternly. "Maybe. You see, there is a part of witchcraft that deals with the soul, a part that believes the soul can be trapped and held, kept from escaping this earth and into the beyond. That's why a lot of natives are superstitious about having their picture taken. They believe once their image is captured, through magic, their soul can be contained.

"Voodoo works much the same. It's nothing but another form of witchcraft. Practitioners of that art believe their souls can be held to this earth by means of someone collecting nail parin's or hair from them while they're still alive.

"That's what Marilyn had in mind. When she saw the girl was fadin', she snipped one of the girl's long pigtails and kept it to herself. Cast spells on it while the child lay dyin', and again after life had left the child."

"The soul was supposed to be contained within the hair?"

"That's right. It can be restored, in a sense, to some other object through the hair. It's like those voodoo dolls. A bit of hair or nail parin' is collected from the person you want to control, or if not control, maintain the presence of their soul, and it's sewn into those dolls. That way, when the pins are stuck into the doll, the living suffer, and when they die their soul is trapped in the doll for all eternity, or rather as long as the doll with its hair or nail parin's exists."

"So she preserved the hair so she could make a doll and have the little girl live on, in a sense?"

"Something like that."

"Sounds crazy."

"I suppose."

"And what of the little girl's father?"

"Ah, that sonofabitch! He came home to find the little girl dead and buried and the mother mad. But there was that little gold lock of hair, and knowing Marilyn, he figured her intentions."

"Machen," I said slowly. "It was you, was it not? You were the father?"

"I was."

"I'm sorry."

"Don't be. We were both foolish. I was the more foolish. She left her husband for me and I cast her aside. Ignored my own child. I was the fool, a great fool."

"Do you really believe in that stuff about the soul? About the hair and what Marilyn was doing?"

"Better I didn't. A soul once lost from the body would best prefer to be departed I think . . . but love is sometimes a brutal thing."

We just sat there after that. We drank more. Machen smoked his pipe, and about an hour later we went to bed.

There were sounds again, gnawing at the edge of my sleep. The sounds that had always been there, but now, since we had talked of Marilyn, I was less able to drift off into blissful slumber. I kept thinking of those crazy things Machen had said. I remembered, too, those voices I had heard, and the fact that Machen was a ventriloquist, and perhaps, not altogether stable.

But those sounds.

I sat up and opened my eyes. They were coming from below. Voices. Machen's first. ". . . not be the death of you, girl, not at all . . . my only reminder of Marilyn . . ."

And then to my horror. "Let me be, Papa. Let it end." The last had been a little girl's voice, but the words had been bitter and wise beyond the youngness of the tone.

I stepped out of bed and into my trousers, crept to the curtain, and looked on Machen's side.

Nothing, just a lonely cot. I wasn't dreaming. I had heard him all right, and the other voice . . . it had to be that Machen, grieved over what he had done in the past, over Marilyn's death, had taken to speaking to himself in the little girl's voice. All that stuff Marilyn had told him about the soul, it had gotten to him, cracked his stability.

I climbed down the cold metal stairs, listening. Below I heard the old, weathered door that led outside slam. Heard the thud of boots going down the outside steps.

I went back up, went to the windows, and pulling back the curtains section by section, finally saw the old man. He was carrying something wrapped in a black cloth and he had a shovel in his hand. I watched as, out there by the shore, he dug a shallow grave and placed the cloth-wrapped object within, placed a rock over it, and left it to the night and the incoming tide.

I pretended to be asleep when he returned, and later, when I felt certain he was well visited by Morpheus, I went downstairs and retrieved the shovel from the tool room. I went out to where I had seen him dig and went to work, first turning over the large stone and shoveling down into the pebbly dirt. Due to the freshness of the hole, it was easy digging.

I found the cloth and what was inside. It made me flinch at first, it looked so real. I thought it was a little rosy-cheeked girl buried alive, for it looked alive . . . but it was a dummy. A ventriloquist dummy. It had aged badly, as if water had gotten to it. In some ways it looked as if it were rotting from the inside out. My finger went easily and deeply into the wood of one of the legs.

Out of some odd curiosity, I reached up and pushed back the wooden eyelids. There were no wooden painted eyes, just darkness, empty sockets that uncomfortably reminded me of looking down into the black hollows of a human skull. And the hair. On one side of the head was a yellow pigtail, but where the other should have been was a bare spot, as if the hair had been ripped away from the wooden skull.

With a trembling hand I closed the lids down over those

empty eyes, put the dirt back in place, the rock, and returned to bed. But I did not sleep well. I dreamed of a grown man talking to a wooden doll and using another voice to answer back, pretending that the doll lived and loved him too.

But the water had gotten to it, and the sight of those rotting legs had snapped him back to reality, dashed his insane hopes of containing a soul by magic, shocked him brutally from foolish dreams. Dead is dead.

The next day, Machen was silent and had little to say. I suspected the events of last night weighed on his mind. Our conversation must have returned to him this morning in sober memory, and he, somewhat embarrassed, was reluctant to recall it. He kept to himself down below in the locked room, and I busied myself with my work.

It was night when he came up, and there was a smug look about him, as if he had accomplished some great deed. We spoke a bit, but not of witches, of past times and the sea. Then he pulled back the curtains and looked at the moon rise above the water like a cold fish eye.

"Machen," I said, "maybe I shouldn't say anything, but if you should ever have something bothering you. If you should ever want to talk about it . . . Well, feel free to come to me."

He smiled at me. "Thank you. But any problem that might have been bothering me is . . . shall we say, all sewn up."

We said little more and soon went to bed.

I slept sounder that night, but again I was rousted from my dreams by voices. Machen's voice again, and the poor man speaking in that little child's voice.

"It's a fine home for you," Machen said in his own voice.

"I want no home," came the little girl's voice. "I want to be free."

"You want to stay with me, with the living. You're just not thinking. There's only darkness beyond the veil."

The voices were very clear and loud. I sat up in bed and strained my ears.

"It's where I belong," the little girl's voice again, but it spoke not in a little girl manner. There was only the tone.

"Things have been bad lately," Machen said. "And you're not yourself."

Laughter, horrible little girl laughter.

"I haven't been myself for years."

"Now, Catherine . . . play your piano. You used to play it so well. Why, you haven't touched it in years."

"Play. Play. With these!"

"You're too loud."

"I don't care. Let him hear, let him . . ."

A door closed sharply and the sound died off to a mumble; a word caught here and there was scattered and confused by the throb of the sea.

Next morning Machen had nothing for me, not even a smile from his borrowed collection. Nothing but coldness, his back, and a frown.

I saw little of him after coffee, and once, from below—for he stayed down there the whole day through—I thought I heard him cry in a loud voice, "Have it your way then," and then there was the sound of a slamming door and some other sort of commotion below.

After a while I looked out at the land and the sea, and down there, striding back and forth, hands behind his back, went Machen, like some great confused penguin contemplating the far shore.

I like to think there was something more than curiosity in what I did next. Like to think I was looking for the source of my friend's agony; looking for some way to help him find peace.

I went downstairs and pulled at the door he kept locked, hoping that, in his anguish, he had forgotten to lock it back. He had not forgotten.

I pressed my ear against the door and listened. Was that crying I heard?

No. I was being susceptible, caught up in Machen's fantasy. It was merely the wind whipping about the tower.

I went back upstairs, had coffee, and wrote not a line.

So day fell into night, and I could not sleep but finally got the strange business out of my mind by reading a novel. A rollicking good sea story of daring men and bloody battles, great ships clashing in a merciless sea.

And then, from his side of the curtain, I heard Machen creak off his cot and take to the stairs. One flight below was the door that led to the railing round about the tower, and I heard that open and close.

I rose, folded a small piece of paper into my book for a marker, and pulled back one of the window curtains. I walked around pulling curtains and looking until I could see him below.

He stood with his hands behind his back, looking out at the sea like a stern father keeping an eye on his children. Then, calmly, he mounted the railing and leaped out into the air.

I ran. Not that it mattered, but I ran, out to the railing . . . and looked down. His body looked like a rag doll splayed on the rocks.

There was no question in my mind that he was dead, but slowly I wound my way down the steps . . . and was distracted by the room. The door stood wide open.

I don't know what compelled me to look in, but I was drawn to it. It was a small room with a desk and a lot of shelves filled with books, mostly occult and black magic. There were carpentry tools on the wall, and all manner of needles and devices that might be used by a tailor. The air was filled with an odd odor I could not place, and on Machen's desk, something that was definitely not tobacco smoldered away.

There was another room beyond the one in which I stood. The door to it was cracked open. I pushed it back and stepped inside. It was a little child's room filled thick with toys and such: jack-in-the-boxes, dolls, kid books, and a toy piano. All were covered in dust.

On the bed lay a teddy bear. It was ripped open and the stuffing was pulled out. There was one long strand of hair hanging out of that gutted belly, just one, as if it were the last morsel of a greater whole. It was the color of honey from a fresh-robbed hive. I knew what the smell in the ashtray was now.

I took the hair and put a match to it, just in case.

:::

Not From Detroit

. . . .

*The inspiration for this one was stolen from a scene in
THE NIGHTRUNNERS. That scene became a short story that
appeared in a literary magazine under the title "A Car
Drives By." Before the book came out, I reread that section
and liked it, but hated the way it was written. I rewrote it,
and in the process came up with a variation for a treatment
for a teleplay. Richard Matheson was the story editor at that
time for AMAZING STORIES, a Spielberg production, and his
son, Richard Christian Matheson, suggested I send it to his
father to see what he thought. I did. Mr. Matheson liked it
and suggested the song at the end of the story. I like to lie
and say I collaborated with Richard Matheson, one of my
heroes. It's stretching the point, but let me have it, okay?*

*Anyway, I rewrote the treatment, and it didn't fly at
AMAZING STORIES, so I worked it into a short story. It
appeared first in* Midnight Graffiti *some time later, and
here it is again.*

*With thanks to Richard Matheson
and Richard Christian Matheson*

Outside it was cold and wet and windy. The storm rattled
the shack, slid like razor blades through the window, door
and wall cracks, but it wasn't enough to make any difference to the couple. Sitting before the crumbling fireplace in

their creaking rocking chairs, shawls across their knees, fingers entwined, they were warm.

A bucket behind them near the kitchen sink collected water dripping from a hole in the roof.

The drops had long since passed the noisy stage of sounding like steel bolts falling on tin, and were now gentle plops.

The old couple were husband and wife; had been for over fifty years. They were comfortable with one another and seldom spoke. Mostly they rocked and looked at the fire as it flickered shadows across the room.

Finally Margie spoke. "Alex," she said, "I hope I die before you."

Alex stopped rocking. "Did you say what I thought you did?"

"I said, I hope I die before you." She wouldn't look at him, just the fire. "It's selfish, I know, but I hope I do. I don't want to live on with you gone. It would be like cutting out my heart and making me walk around. Like one of them zombies."

"There are the children," he said. "If I died, they'd take you in."

"I'd just be in the way. I love them, but I don't want to do that. They got their own lives. I'd just as soon die before you. That would make things simple."

"Not simple for me," Alex said. "I don't want you to die before me. So how about that? We're both selfish, aren't we?"

She smiled. "Well, it ain't a thing to talk about before bedtime, but it's been on my mind, and I had to get it out."

"Been thinking on it too, honey. Only natural we would. We ain't spring chickens anymore."

"You're healthy as a horse, Alex Brooks. Mechanic work you did all your life kept you strong. Me, I got the bursitis and the miseries and I'm tired all the time. Got the old age bad.''

Alex started rocking again. They stared into the fire. ''We're going to go together, hon,'' he said. ''I feel it. That's the way it ought to be for folks like us.''

''I wonder if I'll see him coming. Death, I mean.''

''What?''

''My grandma used to tell me she seen him the night her daddy died.''

''You've never told me this.''

''Ain't a subject I like. But Grandma said this man in a black buggy slowed down out front of their house, cracked his whip three times, and her daddy was gone in instants. And she said she'd heard her grandfather tell how he had seen Death when he was a boy. Told her it was early morning and he was up, about to start his chores, and when he went outside he seen this man dressed in black walk by the house and stop out front. He was carrying a stick over his shoulder with a checkered bundle tied to it, and he looked at the house and snapped his fingers three times. A moment later they found my grandfather's brother, who had been sick with the smallpox, dead in bed.''

''Stories, hon. Stories. Don't get yourself worked up over a bunch of old tall tales. Here, I'll heat us some milk.''

Alex stood, laid the shawl in the chair, went over to put milk in a pan and heat it. As he did, he turned to watch Margie's back. She was still staring into the fire, only she wasn't rocking. She was just watching the blaze, and Alex knew, thinking about dying.

After the milk they went to bed, and soon Margie was asleep, snoring like a busted chainsaw. Alex found he could not rest. It was partly due to the storm, it had picked up in intensity. But it was mostly because of what Margie had said about dying. It made him feel lonesome.

Like her, he wasn't so much afraid of dying, as he was of

being left alone. She had been his heartbeat for fifty years, and without her, he would only be going through motions of life, not living.

God, he prayed silently. When we go, let us go together.

He turned to look at Margie. Her face looked unlined and strangely young. He was glad she could turn off most anything with sleep. He, on the other hand, could not.

Maybe I'm just hungry.

He slid out of bed, pulled on his pants, shirt and houseshoes; those silly things with the rabbit face and ears his granddaughter had bought him. He padded silently to the kitchen. It was not only the kitchen, it served as a den, living room, and dining room. The house was only three rooms and a closet, and one of the rooms was a small bathroom. It was times like this that Alex thought he could have done better by Margie. Gotten her a bigger house, for one thing. It was the same house where they had raised their kids, the babies sleeping in a crib here in the kitchen.

He sighed. No matter how hard he had worked, he seemed to stay in the same place. A poor place.

He went to the refrigerator and took out a half-gallon of milk, drank directly from the carton.

He put the carton back and watched the water drip into the bucket. It made him mad to see it. He had let the little house turn into a shack since he retired, and there was no real excuse for it. Surely, he wasn't that tired. It was a wonder Margie didn't complain more.

Well, there was nothing to do about it tonight. But he vowed that when dry weather came, he wouldn't forget about it this time. He'd get up there and fix that damn leak.

Quietly, he rummaged a pan from under the cabinet. He'd have to empty the bucket now if he didn't want it to run over before morning. He ran a little water into the pan before substituting it for the bucket so the drops wouldn't sound so loud.

He opened the front door, went out on the porch, carrying the bucket. He looked out at his mud-pie yard and his old, red wrecker, his white logo on the side of the door faded with time: ALEX BROOKS WRECKING AND MECHANIC SERVICE.

Tonight, looking at the old warhorse, he felt sadder than ever. He missed using it the way it was meant to be used. For work. Now it was nothing more than transportation. Before he retired, his tools and hands made a living. Now nothing. Picking up a Social Security check was all that was left.

Leaning over the edge of the porch, he poured the water into the bare and empty flower bed. When he lifted his head and looked at his yard again, and beyond to Highway 59, he saw a light. Headlights, actually, looking fuzzy in the rain, like filmed-over amber eyes. They were way out there on the highway, coming from the south, winding their way toward him, moving fast.

Alex thought that whoever was driving that crate was crazy. Cruising like that on bone-dry highways with plenty of sunshine would have been dangerous, but in this weather, they were asking for a crackup.

As the car neared, he could see it was long, black and strangely shaped. He'd never seen anything like it, and he knew cars fairly well. This didn't look like something off the assembly line from Detroit. It had to be foreign.

Miraculously, the car slowed without so much as a quiver or screech of brakes and tires. In fact, Alex could not even hear its motor, just the faint whispering sound of rubber on wet cement.

The car came even of the house just as lightning flashed, and in that instant, Alex got a good look at the driver, or at least the shape of the driver outlined in the flash, and he saw that it was a man with a cigar in his mouth and a bowler hat on his head. And the head was turning toward the house.

The lightning flash died, and now there was only the dark shape of the car and the red tip of the cigar jutting at the house. Alex felt stalactites of ice dripping down from the roof of his skull, extended through his body and out of the soles of his feet.

The driver hit down on his horn; three sharp blasts that pricked at Alex's mind.

Honk. *(visions of blooming roses, withering going black)*

Honk. *(funerals remembered, loved ones in boxes, going down)*

Honk. *(worms crawling through rotten flesh)*

Then came a silence louder than the horn blasts. The car picked up speed again. Alex watched as its taillights winked away in the blackness. The chill became less chill. The stalactites in his mind melted away.

But as he stood there, Margie's words of earlier that evening came at him in a rush: "Seen Death once . . . buggy slowed down out front . . . cracked his whip *three times* . . . man looked at the house, snapped his fingers *three times* . . . found dead a moment later . . ."

Alex's throat felt as if a pine knot had lodged there. The bucket slipped from his fingers, clattered on the porch and rolled into the flowerbed. He turned into the house and walked briskly toward the bedroom,

(Can't be, just a wives' tale)

his hands vibrating with fear.

(Just a crazy coincidence)

Margie wasn't snoring.

Alex grabbed her shoulder, shook her.

Nothing.

He rolled her on her back and screamed her name.

Nothing.

"Oh, baby. No."

He felt for her pulse.

None.

He put an ear to her chest, listening for a heartbeat (the other half of his life bongos), and there was none.

Quiet. Perfectly quiet.

"You can't . . ." Alex said. "You can't. . . . We're suppose to go together . . . Got to be that way."

And then it came to him. He had *seen* Death drive by, had *seen* him heading on down the highway.

He came to his feet, snatched his coat from the back of the chair, raced toward the front door. "You won't have her," he said aloud. "You won't."

Grabbing the wrecker keys from the nail beside the door, he leaped to the porch and dashed out into the cold and the rain.

A moment later he was heading down the highway, driving fast and crazy in pursuit of the strange car.

The wrecker was old and not built for speed, but since he kept it well tuned and it had new tires, it ran well over the wet highway. Alex kept pushing the pedal gradually until it met the floor. Faster and faster and faster.

After an hour, he saw Death.

Not the man himself but the license plate. Personalized and clear in his headlights. It read: DEATH/EXEMPT.

The wrecker and the strange black car were the only ones on the road. Alex closed in on him, honked his horn. Death tootled back (not the same horn sound he had given in front of Alex's house), stuck his arm out the window and waved the wrecker around.

Alex went, and when he was alongside the car, he turned his head to look at Death. He could still not see him clearly, but he could make out the shape of his bowler, and when Death turned to look at him, he could see the glowing tip of the cigar, like a bloody bullet wound.

Alex whipped hard right into the car, and Death swerved to the right, then back onto the road. Alex rammed again. The black car's tires hit roadside gravel and Alex swung closer, preventing it from returning to the highway. He rammed yet another time, and the car went into the grass alongside the road, skidded and went sailing down an embankment and into a tree.

Alex braked carefully, backed off the road and got out of the wrecker. He reached a small pipe wrench and a big crescent wrench out from under the seat, slipped the pipe wrench into his coat pocket for insurance, then went charging down the embankment waving the crescent.

Death opened his door and stepped out. The rain had subsided and the moon was peeking through the clouds like a shy child through gossamer curtains. Its light hit Death's round pink face and made it look like a waxed pomegranate. His cigar hung from his mouth by a tobacco strand.

Glancing up the embankment, he saw an old but strong-looking black man brandishing a wrench and wearing bunny slippers, charging down at him.

Spitting out the ruined cigar, Death stepped forward, grabbed Alex's wrist and forearm, twisted. The old man went up and over, the wrench went flying from his hand. Alex came down hard on his back, the breath bursting out of him in spurts.

Death leaned over Alex. Up close, Alex could see that the pink face was slightly pocked and that some of the pinkness was due to makeup. That was rich. Death was vain about his appearance. He was wearing a black T-shirt, pants and sneakers, and of course his derby, which had neither been stirred by the wreck nor by the ju-jitsu maneuver.

"What's with you, man?" Death asked.

Alex wheezed, tried to catch his breath. "You . . . can't . . . have . . . her."

"Who? What are you talking about?"

"Don't play . . . dumb with me." Alex raised up on one elbow, his wind returning. "You're Death and you took my Margie's soul."

Death straightened. "So you know who I am. All right. But what of it? I'm only doing my job."

"It ain't her time."

"My list says it is, and my list is never wrong."

Alex felt something hard pressing against his hip, realized what it was. The pipe wrench. Even the throw Death had put on him had not hurled it from his coat pocket. It had lodged there and the pocket had shifted beneath his hip, making his old bones hurt all the worse.

Alex made as to roll over, freed the pocket beneath him, shot his hand inside and produced the pipe wrench. He hurled it at Death, struck him just below the brim of the bowler and sent him stumbling back. This time the bowler fell off. Death's forehead was bleeding.

Before Death could collect himself, Alex was up and rushing. He used his head as a battering ram and struck Death in the stomach, knocking him to the ground. He put both knees on Death's arms, pinning them, clenched his throat with his strong, old hands.

"I ain't never hurt nobody before," Alex said. "Don't want to now. I didn't want to hit you with that wrench, but you give Margie back."

Death's eyes showed no expression at first, but slowly a light seemed to go on behind them. He easily pulled his arms out from under Alex's knees, reached up, took hold of the old man's wrist and pulled the hands away from his throat.

"You old rascal," Death said. "You outsmarted me."

Death flopped Alex over on his side, then stood up. Grinning, he turned, stooped to recover his bowler, but he never laid a hand on it.

Alex moved like a crab, scissoring his legs, and caught Death from above and behind his knees, twisted, brought him down on his face.

Death raised up on his palms and crawled from behind

Alex's legs like a snake, effortlessly. This time he grabbed the hat and put it on his head and stood up. He watched Alex carefully.

"I don't frighten you much, do I?" Death asked.

Alex noted that the wound on Death's forehead had vanished. There wasn't even a drop of blood. "No," Alex said. "You don't frighten me much. I just want my Margie back."

"All right," Death said.

Alex sat bolt upright.

"What?"

"I said, all right. For a time. Not many have outsmarted me, pinned me to the ground. I give you credit, and you've got courage. I like that. I'll give her back. For a time. Come here."

Death walked over to the car that was not from Detroit. Alex got to his feet and followed. Death took the keys out of the ignition, moved to the trunk, worked the key in the lock. It popped up with a hiss.

Inside were stacks and stacks of matchboxes. Death moved his hand over them, like a careful man selecting a special vegetable at the supermarket. His fingers came to rest on a matchbox that looked to Alex no different than the others.

Death handed Alex the matchbox. "Her soul's in here, old man. You stand over her bed, open the box. Okay?"

"That's it?"

"That's it. Now get out of here before I change my mind. And remember, I'm giving her back to you. But just for a while."

Alex started away, holding the matchbox carefully. As he walked past Death's car, he saw the dents he had knocked in the side with his wrecker were popping out. He turned to look at Death, who was closing the trunk.

"Don't suppose you'll need a tow out of here?"

Death smiled thinly. "Not hardly."

Alex stood over their bed; the bed where they had loved, slept, talked and dreamed. He stood there with the matchbox in his hand, his eyes on Margie's cold face. He ever so gently eased the box open. A small flash of blue light, like Peter Pan's friend Tinkerbell, rushed out of it and hit Margie's lips. She made a sharp inhaling sound and her chest rose. Her eyes came open. She turned and looked at Alex and smiled.

"My lands, Alex. What are you doing there, and half-dressed? What have you been up to . . . is that a matchbox?"

Alex tried to speak, but he found that he could not. All he could do was grin.

"Have you gone nuts?" she asked.

"Maybe a little." He sat down on the bed and took her hand. "I love you, Margie."

"And I love you . . . You been drinking?"

"No."

Then came the overwhelming sound of Death's horn. One harsh blast that shook the house, and the headbeams shone brightly through the window and the cracks lit up the shack like a cheap nightclub act.

"Who in the world?" Margie asked.

"Him. But he said . . . Stay here."

Alex got his shotgun out of the closet. He went out on the porch. Death's car was pointed toward the house, and the headbeams seemed to hold Alex, like a fly in butter.

Death was standing on the bottom step, waiting.

Alex pointed the shotgun at him. "You git. You gave her back. You gave your word."

"And I kept it. But I said for a while."

"That wasn't any time at all."

"It was all I could give. My present."

"Short time like that's worse than no time at all."

"Be good about it, Alex. Let her go. I got records and they have to be kept. I'm going to take her anyway, you understand that?"

"Not tonight, you ain't." Alex pulled back the hammers on the shotgun. "Not tomorrow night neither. Not anytime soon."

"That gun won't do you any good, Alex. You know that. You can't stop Death. I can stand here and snap my fingers three times, or click my tongue, or go back to the car and honk my horn, and she's as good as mine. But I'm trying to reason with you, Alex. You're a brave man. I did you a favor because you bested me. I didn't want to just take her back without telling you. That's why I came here to talk. But she's got to go. Now."

Alex lowered the shotgun. "Can't . . . can't you take me in her place? You can do that, can't you?"

"I . . . I don't know. It's highly irregular."

"Yeah, you can do that. Take me. Leave Margie."

"Well, I suppose."

The screen door creaked open and Margie stood there in her housecoat. "You're forgetting, Alex, I don't want to be left alone."

"Go in the house, Margie," Alex said.

"I know who this is: I heard you talking, Mr. Death. I don't want you taking my Alex. I'm the one you came for. I ought to have the right to go."

There was a pause, no one speaking. Then Alex said, "Take both of us. You can do that, can't you? I know I'm on that list of yours, and pretty high up. Man my age couldn't have too many years left. You can take me a little before my time, can't you? Well, can't you?"

*   *   *

Margie and Alex sat in their rocking chairs, their shawls over their knees. There was no fire in the fireplace. Behind them the bucket collected water and outside the wind whistled. They held hands. Death stood in front of them. He was holding a King Edward cigar box.

"You're sure of this?" Death asked. "You don't both have to go."

Alex looked at Margie, then back at Death.

"We're sure," he said. "Do it."

Death nodded. He opened the cigar box and held it out on one palm. He used his free hand to snap his fingers.

Once. *(the wind picked up, howled)*

Twice. *(the rain beat like drumsticks on the roof)*

Three times. *(lightning ripped and thunder roared)*

"And in you go," Death said.

The bodies of Alex and Margie slumped and their heads fell together between the rocking chairs. Their fingers were still entwined.

Death put the box under his arm and went out to the car. The rain beat on his derby hat and the wind sawed at his bare arms and T-shirt. He didn't seem to mind.

Opening the trunk, he started to put the box inside, then hesitated.

He closed the trunk.

"Damn," he said, "if I'm not getting to be a sentimental old fool."

He opened the box. Two blue lights rose out of it, elongated, touched ground. They took on the shape of Alex and Margie. They glowed against the night.

"Want to ride up front?" Death asked.

"That would be nice," Margie said.

"Yes, nice," Alex said.

Death opened the door and Alex and Margie slid inside. Death climbed in behind the wheel. He checked the clipboard dangling from the dash. There was a woman in a

Tyler hospital, dying of brain damage. That would be his next stop.

He put the clipboard down and started the car that was not from Detroit.

"Sounds well-tuned," Alex said.

"I try to keep it that way," Death said.

They drove out of there then, and as they went, Death broke into song. "Row, row, row your boat, gently down the stream," and Margie and Alex chimed in with "Merrily, merrily, merrily, merrily, life is but a dream."

Off they went down the highway, the taillights fading, the song dying, the black metal of the car melting into the fabric of night, and then there was only the whispery sound of good tires on wet cement and finally not even that. Just the blowing sound of the wind and the rain.

Pentecostal
Punk Rock

Another story I have very little memory of.

Let me just say I have this thing about religion, and generally speaking, it's a negative thing. Our neighbors were zealous Pentecostals, the husband being a failed musician and a failed liquor salesman who had found God and opened a church across from us, and later, ever so briefly, a Gospel Opry which was advertised along our road by giant, orange Day-Glo guitars that at night seemed to float in the air, pointing the way to the Opry.

Anyway, they thought we were weird, and we thought they were weird. Certainly, for us, they were a constant source of amusement. But that's a long story. Let me just say that this story was probably influenced by something that happened across the way, some little incident that I combined with a rainy season and something I thought would be totally incongruous to the Pentecostal lifestyle— Punk Rock.

It appeared some years after it was written, like a number of my stories. It's sort of transitional, like a couple other stories here, and for that reason I have a soft spot for it. Outside of that, I don't remember much about the actual writing. Stories like this, however, always make me suspicion popcorn.

For Robert Bloch

Ira Finney never expected the girl at his apartment door to be selling religion. Begging, perhaps, or ringing the wrong doorbell, but peddling God was a surprise. She claimed to be a Pentecostal, but he had never seen a Punk Rock Pentecostal before. She had orange hair with a shaved spot on the right side of her head and her clothes were a mixed bag; oversized sweater, a plaid skirt, one white sock (the other foot was sockless) and what looked like plastic rain shoes. Over her shoulder was a plastic rain coat. There hadn't been a sign of rain in weeks.

Under her arm was something large and flat, and clutched in her fist like a club, was a roll of tracts. She pushed the roll at him.

"Here," she said.

He was intrigued. He took one. Glancing at the face of it, he saw that it read: *Pentecostal Punk Rock, the Wave of the Future, So Get Your Shit Together.*

He looked at the girl and smiled. She was chewing gum, but she smiled back. She was oddly attractive. Like a cute mongrel mutt. And having been separated from his wife for a year now, and having spent many lonely nights without so much as a look at a woman, improved her looks, made him feel brave.

"Why don't you come in and tell me about it."

"Not much to tell," she said, coming inside, looking around while she popped her gum. "It's all in the paper there."

"Don't you want to make a convert?"

She shrugged. "Yeah, sure, but we don't work for it. I gave you the tract, that's enough. You got your chance. You don't pay attention, ain't my fault. You'll get yours when the big flood comes."

Ira smiled. The girl was obviously unaware of the Bible. The Flood was the first time God destroyed the world. Next time, according to The Bible, destruction would be by fire. He didn't say anything to that effect, however.

"Well, if you don't work to make converts, how come you came inside?"

She smiled. "Wanted to see how somebody like you lived."

"And?"

"All right."

Ira used his smile again. He was going to try and put the move on this girl. She looked like the type that had been around, and might want to go around once more. She also looked like someone who wouldn't expect any ties, any real emotional involvement. And though he didn't like to think it so bluntly, what he needed at the moment was simple. Sex.

"What's that under your arm?" he asked. "A book?"

"Sounds," she said, and handed it to him for a look. It was a record album. It was called *Pentecostal Punk Rock: Pogo Out*. It was by some group called The Destruction.

"Perhaps we could hear it?" he said.

She smiled. "Hey, man, you trying to put the make on me?"

"I'm working at it."

The smile got bigger. "Maybe that's all right. You're kind of cute for a straight. I ain't saying it's all right, now. I'm just saying maybe, got me?"

"Yeah, I got you."

"This kind of music doesn't look like your scene, man," she said.

"Does this religion?" he said, holding up the tract.

"No, but you got to try, you know. God and his work and all that crap."

"I see. You been canvassing long?"

"What?"

"Going door to door?"

"Oh. Just since I became a true believer. About a month ago."

"Is this branch of the Pentecostal church new?"

"I'll say. Brand new. The other Pentecostals don't have a thing to do with us. They say we're crazy and don't know what's up. But they don't have a clue, man. They won't be crowing so loud when the flood comes."

"I see."

"Hey, you wanna hear those sounds, or not?"

"Sure."

He put the album on the stereo and waved her to the couch. She sat on one end and he sat on the other. He looked at her and smiled. She smiled back and glided down the couch to sit next to him. She tossed the raincoat off her shoulder onto the floor, dropped the tracts on top of it. He let his arm slip around her shoulders. She didn't seem to mind. It felt very good to have his arm around a woman. It had been a long time.

The music started, if you could call it that. It sounded like a recording of car wrecks, train derailments and plane crashes set to music.

After a minute of this, the girl, overcome, leaped to her feet and started bounding and flailing about the room. It didn't look so much like dancing, as it looked like she was struggling with an invisible opponent.

The music built.

The girl began to chant under her breath. Some of it sounded like Bible verses, most of it nonsense. Suddenly she stopped and looked at him.

"Hey, you're not digging the sounds."

"Well," he admitted, "it's not my thing."

"I can see that. Well, too bad."

She leaned over and kissed him. He kissed her back, and the kisses got hotter and hotter. His hands explored, and hers returned the favor. The music beat like a struggling heart in the background.

Pretty soon their clothes were off and they were flopping around on the couch like spawning salmon. The first time it ended quickly, in a passionate rush. The second and third time took longer and was sweeter. After that, she turned over the album, which seemed nearly endless, and they retired to the bedroom.

It had grown dark and he turned on the lamp next to his bedside. It had small wattage and provided a pleasant light for lovemaking. And strangely, it was by this dim light that he first really took note of her body. She was astride him, head tilted up in ecstasy. From that angle he could see the rapid pulse in her smooth neck and the pointed tip of her chin. He could see the bottoms of her eyes, and they were expressionless, bulged out, as if she were being pumped up with air. From his angle they looked lidless.

Her body was sleek, lean and boyish. Her breasts little more than bee-stings. Her white flesh, especially the small bulge of her belly, reminded him of the underside of a fish. For some reason he suddenly felt nauseous with her, as if he had eaten something bad and not until this moment realized it.

He was more than happy when the music finished, and she with it. She lay beside him and fell fast asleep.

Lying there, no longer straining with passion, she looked quite different. More feminine. But her flesh felt clammy and the sweat that clung to her was in large beads and smelled heavily of salt. It was like breathing beach air. He found he could not lie beside her.

Rolling out of bed, he put on his robe and padded to the living room, turned on the light. He sat down on the couch and wished now that he had never let her in. He hoped she would depart tomorrow without trouble. He hoped, too, she wouldn't want an encore.

Idly, he reached over and picked up one of the tracts, opened it.

The contents were strange indeed. No wonder the Pentecostals didn't claim them. Who would?

Mixed with Punk lore and band reviews were excerpts from The Bible and a mass of strange letters and designs that looked akin to Egyptian hieroglyphics. There were also newspaper extracts about violent crimes, a few graphic photos of victims of maiming accidents, murders, and rapes.

Finney felt repulsed, but curiosity caused him to examine it closer. He couldn't decide from the tracts if the Punker sect was opposed to these things, for them, or just damn indifferent.

As he read, he realized that the girl's statements about the flood were not entirely out of whack. At least not with her religion. The flood of old, as well as the story of Jonah being swallowed by a great fish, were of considerable importance to the Punkers. In fact, comments about water occurred over and over again in the tract. And as for the Biblical prediction of the second destruction of the world being caused by fire, the Punkers were in total opposition. They said God had changed His mind, and Acid-Face Ronnie knew the score.

Acid-Face Ronnie was the prophet of the Punk Rock Pentecostals. It was his contention that God had spoken to him personally, and had assured him that a flood was going to be the way the world went out this time as well, and all the old bets were off. Acid-Face Ronnie claimed it was like when the Old Testament was out and the New Testament was in. Only now this was the New New Testament (referring to the tract, Finney took it), and those who did not heed its warning were going to be "drowned suckers."

God was bored with the whole human race thing and was all out of the forgiving mood. It was survival of the fittest, and it was time to heed God's new law or face the big, deep wash.

The album was mentioned in the tract. It was part of what helped you prepare for the flood. It *was* the sound of car wrecks, train derailments, plane crashes and the like set to music. There were also, the tract claimed, the screams of the injured and the dying on it.

A cold chill wriggled its way up Ira's back. He wondered how the Punkers could have come by such recordings. He hoped it was all hype. The idea of cold-bloodedly causing those things to happen so they could be taped made the hair on the back of his neck bristle. Surely it was all a hoax; something to go with their unconventional lifestyle.

Skipping to another page, he found something about becoming one with water, but he couldn't make sense of it. It seemed the Pentecostal Punkers thought that if you danced to their album, doing a thing called The Pogo, recited certain Bible verses, as well as verses provided in the tract by Acid-Face Ronnie, you could hope to survive.

His thoughts were interrupted by the sound of thunder. It was loud and reverberating, like someone slamming a baseball bat against a sheet of tin.

It was then that he noticed the walls were bleeding great drops of condensation.

Ira got up and touched the wall. It was damp and cold and smelled bad, like rotting seaweed.

Thunder rumbled again.

He went to the window, drew the curtain, looked down from his twelve story apartment in the city. It was raining briskly and the neon lights below made everything look distorted. The buildings all seemed under water, like stalagmites beneath the sea. The neon lights were like colored coral, and the lights of cars like the glowing eyes of small, scuttling fish.

He rubbed his tired eyes, and just as he brought his hands

down, he thought he saw something dart by his window. It had been so fast, it was nearly subliminal, but he couldn't help but think what he'd seen was a man. A Punker with a mohawk making swimming motions against the night sky. A Punker who was part human and part. . . .

He shook his head, as if to clear it of obstructions. He could not have seen anything. That was preposterous. He was twelve stories up. People did not swim in the air, and they certainly did not look like that—a Punker with a fin on his back, and in place of legs, a long, flickering fish tail.

Leaning on the glass, Ira tried to look around the corner of the building, but the angle prevented such nonsense. He saw nothing more out of the ordinary, and realized he had seen nothing in the first place. He had Punk Rockers on the brain.

He laughed, but it was more of a rattle than a laugh.

He found himself drawn back to the couch and the crazy tract. He flipped back to the part on how to survive, cruised again over the section dealing with the album, the chanting and the dancing. There were also warning signs listed for the end of the world. The usual stuff. Violence in the streets. Nations squabbling. Things that were difficult to be accurate about.

Then it got down to more immediate concerns.

There would be a prophet (Acid-Face Ronnie, of course). The prophet would spread the word—quickly, because there wasn't much time. Some would listen, most wouldn't. The prophet was not to sweat those who didn't. His job was to spread the word, not worry about its acceptance. God had told him to tell his friends and relatives first, then others. Then, in the month of December. . . .

Ira paused in his reading. My God, he thought, today is December the 12th.

. . . it would begin to rain, suddenly, after a long dry spell. There would be the smell of the sea, and all things, animate or inanimate, would forecast their watery future to those who had heard the word, even if they had not accepted its truth. They would have visions of the future; visions of the world's doom.

Scanning more of the tract, he found greater detail on surviving. The chanting, dancing and such, supposedly allowed the true believer to "become one with the flood," whatever that meant. And those who didn't become one with the flood would drown and become food for the survivors.

He let that idea bounce around inside his head for a moment.

Good God, they were talking about cannibalism. Living off the drowned or the drowning. It was repulsive.

Continuing to read, he found that even believing did not guarantee survival. One's degree of strength and protection had to do with one's degree of belief and commitment. Levels of belief had levels of award.

Enough.

He tossed the tract aside. He was getting as crazy as the girl and this nut, Acid-Face Ronnie. He was starting to consider this stuff.

Sure, the wall bled smelly water, but that was nothing prophetic. Maybe a nest of rats had eaten away the insulation and something in it had killed them. Then it rained after a long dry spell, and with it being a cold December . . . Well, the weather could have caused condensation and carried the stink of the dead rodents into his apartment by route of water beads. A little farfetched, but possible. Certainly it made more sense than that garbage in the tract.

Albums of destruction set to rock music? Cannibalism? A God that saw the world as a cosmic joke and decided to mix the old rules with some new ones, then give them all to a crazed Punk Rocker and send him out to form his own religion?

It just didn't add up.

As for the vision at the window . . . hallucination. Couldn't have been anything else. He was overly tired and maybe the intensity of the sex act after such a long dry spell had something to do with it. Farfetched again, but still more in the ball park than Pentecostal Punk Rock.

Or maybe the girl had slipped him something? That was a strong possibility. Her type was always taking something, and the way she had looked when they made love; the oddness of her eyes.

But they hadn't drunk or eaten a thing, so how would it have been passed to him? Kissing? Were there some drugs that could be passed that way? Her kisses had tasted strange, like . . . like the after lurk of a bad oyster dinner.

That was crazy. Drugs passed by kissing? It made no sense.

He felt a tide of queasiness pound its surf against him and he hung his head between his knees to let it pass.

It did, but not fully.

He rose, went to the bathroom and splashed water on his face. His reflection in the mirror was very pale.

Leaning forward, he pushed the top of his head against the mirror and stared into the sink. The water was still running, and as he idly reached to turn it off, a great glob of seaweed oozed out of the faucet and plopped into the sink. This was followed by molasses-thick mud and small, shiny fish. The fish flapped their tails weakly in the muck. The smell of seaweed and fish filled his nostrils.

Ira threw up in the sink.

Lifting his head, he saw his reflection in the watery mirror. The muscles in his face jumped, as if firecrackers had exploded beneath his face. His cheeks were equipped with gills and scales. He would have screamed, but he was too shocked to find his voice.

He closed the lid on the john and sat down there, dizzy, confused.

It was true. The Punk Rockers were onto it. The end of the world was coming by flood, and he, who had been introduced to it by the girl and the tracts, was having visions of the future, and it was a depressing one.

The album. Had to play it. Had to chant and dance. If he was going to survive, he had to do that. There was that thing about levels of believing, and though he was having a hard time believing any of this, he had to be ready when the flood came.

Standing, he chanced a glance into the mirror. His face was back to normal. The only thing in the sink was vomit. He turned on the water. No fish came out. He let it run until the vomit washed down the drain.

His new-found faith backslid. Maybe it was all a hallucination.

But at that moment, lightning cracked loudly and the air was filled with the smell of ozone and rotting fish. It practically raped his nostrils.

He darted into the living room, put on the album, turned up the volume. He grabbed the tract off the floor and found the verses.

The music started and he began to dance, trying to copy the way the girl had moved. He read the tract as he danced, which wasn't easy. He stumbled over the words, having to stop dancing every few seconds to read them better, push them into memory. Then he'd resume his pogoing, reciting what he had memorized.

As he bobbed up and down, the stink of the sea and ozone increased. Rain began to rattle against the windows and roof.

The bedroom door opened, and the girl, naked, came

dancing and smiling into the room. Her arms and legs gyrated wildly, like the limbs of a spider being electrocuted. Her mouth opened and the chanting rolled out. She jumped over the back of the couch, landed on the cushions, kicking them to the floor and following after them. She wheeled and leaped about the room. It was wild and graceful at the same time.

Ira, in spite of himself, found his eyes drawn to her nakedness. He saw too that she had that look about her eyes again; the bulging, lidless look.

Ira jerked off his robe, tossed it aside, danced with the girl, the both of them chanting. One moment he felt foolish, the next exhilarated.

Gradually the air became more difficult to breathe. The walls weaved in and out as if great hands were pressing from all sides. A window blew in, sprinkled glass on the carpet. Rain blasted in after it in a torrent. The curtains flapped savagely like the wriggling tongues of snakes tasting air. Ira could see nothing but great darkness outside. The neon made no reflection against the night sky.

The apartment lights went dead, and so did the album, but it was as if he could hear the music in his head. He found to his surprise that his vision had altered and he could see quite well in the dark, even well enough to read the tract. He chanted louder, danced more vigorously to his mental music.

The girl had thrown herself on the cold, wet, glass-sharded carpet and was flapping about like a fish in shallow water. She spun around on her buttocks, and finally popped to her feet, her eyes glowing in the dark, her ass dripping blood from the glass cuts.

Then it all happened at once. The walls turned to wet crepe and the floor rose up and the ceiling came down. Ira found himself swimming into a massive wave of water, plaster and sailing furniture. The tract had slipped from his hand and momentarily plastered itself against his face.

The wave went higher, and he found he could climb it, like a roach scuttling up the side of a toilet bowl.

So up he went, and when the wave washed back in a wet loop and rose up again, he saw between his fast-shriveling legs the flip of his long, scaly tail. And when he reached out to grab water, to swim forward, he saw flippers, not hands, and when the wave pushed him up yet again, he saw rising from the foam the tip of a skyscraper, its copperish windows blinking briefly as an escaped ray from the moon pierced the clouds reflected against it. But that was soon gone, replaced by water. Then he was no longer swimming, but trying to claw his way up the collapsing wall of his apartment. There was the sound of that wild music in his head, as well as the sound of the waves and the storm. He had come unglued for a moment in time and space and had moved backward.

The apartment weaved in and out, and finally the white walls and furniture were replaced by dark water, debris and the screams of the cold, wet, drowning non-believers. And this time he did not shift back in time. There was only the water now, and its wet future. Debris and dead bodies boiled past him.

Torquing his slick, wet body, he looked behind him, saw the girl's face. But the face was like a mask worn by something else. She was big and long, sleek and gray. Her eyes were beginning to slip to the sides of her head, and he found that it was the same in his case. His range of vision was changing.

When he looked again, the girl's lips were projecting forward, falling open to reveal great teeth that crashed against the surf. She swam toward him with an enthusiasm that frightened him, and he immediately knew why. He had survived the flood through belief, same as her, but his was sudden belief, not long held like the girl's. Her chanting and dancing had been going on for some time and she was good at both. He was not.

He remembered what the tract said about the levels of belief and award, and he understood what that meant now. He had become one with the flood by becoming fish-like, and so had she. Only she was a bigger fish. A more powerful and deadly fish.

A hungry fish.

Twisting once to view behind him, he saw that her eyes had slipped completely to the sides of her head, and the only vestiges of humanity left to her were an orange slash of hair on the left side of her skull and a fast-fading bump of a nose that lay dead center of her tooth-filled snout. A sizable dark fin like a flattened pyramid rose from her back.

He tried to scream, but he could not. No vocal cords.

The fin went under and the water went up, carrying him with it, driving him to the summit of a black, wet spire. And as he crashed down, he saw waiting for him the girl—or what she now was. The orange hair patch was now an orange stripe of skin across her bony head and the bump of a nose was gone. She rolled her head to the side to position her bulging eye for a better view of him; opened her mouth to give him a better look at those rows and rows of sharp, dagger teeth. And try as he might to avoid them, he could not. She was too quick, too purposeful.

With a whip of her big, sleek body, she burst up to take his soft head into her hard mouth, and she squeezed down violently, tasting the first of the many lesser species that the Lord had provided for one of his greatest true believers.

The Job

This appeared in RAZORED SADDLES, an anthology I co-edited. I dislike having my own material in a book I'm helping to edit, but Dark Harvest, my publisher, insisted. This story came out. It didn't fit the guidelines of the anthology very well, but I justified it with an introduction as best I could. I didn't lie, but I stretched things a little. That's okay. I dislike strict guidelines anyway.

This one is short and mean and in line with a lot of my more recent fiction as far as tone goes.

For Pat LoBrutto

Bower pulled the sun visor down and looked in the mirror there and said, "You know, hadn't been for the travel, I'd have done all right. I could even shake my ass like him. I tell you, it drove the women wild. You should have seen 'em."

"Don't shake it for me," Kelly said. "I don't want to see it. Things I got to do are tough enough without having to see that."

Bower pushed the visor back. The light turned green. Kelly put the gas to the car and they went up and over a hill and turned right on Melroy.

"Guess maybe you do look like him," Kelly said. "During his fatter days, when he was on the drugs and the peanut butter."

149

"Yeah, but these pocks on my cheeks messes it up some. When I was on stage I had makeup on 'em. I looked okay then."

They stopped at a stop sign and Kelly got out a cigarette and pushed in the lighter.

"A nigger nearly tail-ended me here once," Kelly said. "Just come barreling down on me." He took the lighter and lit his smoke. "Scared the piss out of me. I got him out of his car and popped him some. I bet he was one careful nigger from then on." He pulled away from the stop sign and cruised.

"You done one like this before? I know you've done it, but like this?"

"Not just like this. But I done some things might surprise you. You getting nervous on me?"

"I'm all right. You know, thing made me quit the Elvis imitating was travel, cause one night on the road I was staying in this cheap motel, and it wasn't heated too good. I'd had those kinds of rooms before, and I always carried couple of space heaters in the trunk of the car with the rest of my junk, you know. I got them plugged in, and I was still cold, so I pulled the mattress on the floor by the heaters. I woke up and was on fire. I had been so worn out I'd gone to sleep in my Elvis outfit. That was the end of my best white jumpsuit, you know, like he wore with the gold glitter and all. I must have been funny on fire like that, hopping around the room beating it out. When I got that suit off I was burned like the way you get when you been out in the sun too long."

"You gonna be able to do this?"

"Did I say I couldn't?"

"You're nervous. I can tell way you talk."

"A little. I always get nervous before I go on stage too, but I always come through. Crowd came to see Elvis, by god, they got Elvis. I used to sign autographs with his name. People wanted it like that. They wanted to pretend, see.''

''Women mostly?''

''Uh huh.''

''What were they, say, fifty-five?''

''They were all ages. Some of them were pretty young.''

''Ever fuck any of 'em?''

''Sure, I got plenty. Sing a little Love Me Tender to them in the bedroom and they'd do whatever I wanted.''

''Was it the old ones you was fucking?''

''I didn't fuck no real old ones, no. Whose idea is it to do things this way, anyhow?''

''Boss, of course. You think he lets me plan this stuff? He don't want them chinks muscling in on the shrimping and all.''

''I don't know, we fought for these guys. It seems a little funny.''

''Reason we lost the war over there is not being able to tell one chink from another and all of them being the way they are. I think we should have nuked the whole god-damned place. Went over there when it cooled down and stopped glowing, put in a fucking Disneyland or something.''

They were moving out of the city now, picking up speed.

''I don't see why we don't just whack this guy outright and not do it this way,'' Bower said. ''This seems kind of funny.''

''No one's asking you. You come on a job, you do it. Boss wants some chink to suffer, so he's gonna suffer. Not like he didn't get some warnings or nothing. Boss wants him to take it hard.''

''Maybe this isn't a smart thing on account of it may not bother chinks like it'd bother us. They're different about stuff like this, all the things they've seen.''

''It'll bother him,'' Kelly said. ''And if it don't, that ain't our problem. We got a job to do and we're gonna do it. Whatever comes after comes after. Boss wants us to do different next time, we do different. Whatever he wants we do it. He's the one paying.''

They were out of the city now and to the left of the highway they could see the glint of the sea through a line of scrubby trees.

''How're we gonna know?'' Bower said. ''One chink looks like another.''

''I got a photograph. This one's got a burn scar on the face. Everything's timed. Boss has been planning this. He had some of the guys watch and take notes. It's all set up.''

''Why us?''

''Me because I've done some things before. You because he wants to see what you're made of. I'm kind of here as your nurse maid.''

''I don't need anybody to see that I do what I'm supposed to do.''

They drove past a lot of boats pulled up to a dock. They drove into a small town called Wilborn. They turned a corner at Catlow Street.

''It's down here a ways,'' Kelly said. ''You got your knife? You left your knife and brought your comb, I'm gonna whack you.''

Bower got the knife out of his pocket. ''Thing's got a lot of blades, some utility stuff. Even a comb.''

''Christ, you're gonna do it with a Boy Scout knife?''

''Utility knife. The blade I want is plenty sharp, you'll see. Why couldn't we use a gun? That wouldn't be as messy. A lot easier.''

''Boss wants it messy. He wants the chink to think about it some. He wants them to pack their stuff on their boats and sail back to chink land. Either that, or they can pay their percentages like everyone else. He lets the chinks get away with things, everyone'll want to get away with things.''

They pulled over to the curb. Down the street was a school. Bower looked at his watch.

"Maybe if it was a nigger," Bower said.

"Chink, nigger, what's the difference?"

They could hear a bell ringing. After five minutes they saw kids going out to the curb to get on the buses parked there. A few kids came down the sidewalk toward them. One of them was a Vietnamese girl about eight years old. The left side of her face was scarred.

"Won't they remember me?" Bower said.

"Kids? Naw. Nobody knows you around here. Get rid of that Elvis look and you'll be okay."

"It don't seem right. In front of these kids and all. I think we ought to whack her father."

"No one's paying you to think, Elvis. Do what you're supposed to do. I have to do it and you'll wish you had."

Bower opened the utility knife and got out of the car. He held the knife by his leg and walked around front, leaned on the hood just as the Vietnamese girl came up. He said, "Hey, kid, come here a minute." His voice got thick. "Elvis wants to show you something."

The Events Concerning a Nude Fold-Out Found in a Harlequin Romance

This story, like "The Job", is of more recent vintage. It too appeared in an anthology I co-edited. Again, I don't like the idea of appearing in my own anthologies, but am beginning to realize it's a bargaining chip. I'm amazed I have anything to bargain, but am, of course, delighted.

This story was inspired by Roman Ranieri. During a phone conversation, he told me that he found a men's magazine fold-out in a Harlan Ellison book. He thought that was kind of humorous, and wrote Harlan about it. If memory serves me, Harlan thought it was funny too.

But as soon as Roman told me that story, a light went on. I don't remember if I told him what I had in mind right then, or if it jelled a bit and I called him back. It doesn't matter. It was one of those wonderful writer moments when the concept for a story is so strong you not only know you're going to write it, but that it's going to flow like water over the proverbial dam.

It wasn't my intention for the story to be as long as it is, but I couldn't stop. And I'm glad. It came out pretty nice, I like to think. It shows my goofier side. The story was influenced not only by Roman's anecdote, but by the old Dell Map Back mystery books, forties detective movies that mixed hard-boiled detection and comedy, and Hitchcock films. Add a lot of Joe Lansdale to that, and you get this, the final story in the collection. I hope there will be other stories about Plebin, Martha and Jasmine, a novel maybe. I enjoy their company, as I've enjoyed your company during our little visit here.

Y'all come again. Hear?

For Roman Ranieri

Looking back on it, I wouldn't have thought something as strange as all this, full of the real coincidence of life, would have begun with a bad circus, but that's how it started, at least for me.

My luck had gone from bad to worse, then over the lip of worse, and into whatever lower level it can descend into. My job at the aluminum chair plant had played out and no rich relatives had died and left me any money. Fact was, I don't think the Cooks, least any that are kin to me, have any money, outside of a few quarters to put in a juke box come Saturday night, maybe a few bucks to waste on something like pretzels and beer.

Me, I didn't even have money for beer or juke boxes. I was collecting a little money on unemployment, and I was out beating the bushes for a job, but there didn't seem to be much in the way of work in Mud Creek. I couldn't even get on at the feed store carrying out bags of fertilizer and seed. All the sixteen-year-olds had that job.

It looked like I was going to have to move out of Mud Creek to find work, and though the idea of that didn't hurt my feelings any, there was Jasmine, my teenage daughter, and she still had a year of high school to finish before she went off to Nacogdoches to start her degree in anthropology at Stephen F. Austin State University, and I planned to follow her over there and find a place of my own where we could be near, and improve our relationship, which overall was all right to begin with. I just wanted more time with her.

Right then Jasmine lived with her mother, and her mother

doesn't care a damn for me. She wanted to marry a guy that was going to be a high roller, and believe me, I wanted to be a high roller, but what she got was a guy who each time at the mark throws craps. No matter what I do, it turns to shit. Last break I felt I'd had in life was when I was ten and fell down and cracked my ankle. Well, maybe there was one good break after all. One that wasn't a bone. Jasmine. She's smart and pretty and ambitious and the love of my life.

But my marital problems and life's woes are not what this is about. I was saying about the circus.

It was mid-June, and I'd tried a couple places, looking for work, and hadn't gotten any, and I'd gone over to the employment office to talk to the people there and embarrass myself about not finding any work yet. They told me they didn't have anything for me either, but they didn't look embarrassed at all. When it's you and the employment office, better known as the unemployment office, feeling embarrassed is a one-way street and you're the one driving on it. They seem almost proud to tell you how many unemployment checks you got left, so it can kind of hang over your head like an anvil or something.

So, I thanked them like I meant it and went home, and believe me, that's no treat.

Home is a little apartment about the size of a wash room at a Fina Station, only not as nice and without the air-conditioning. The window looks out over Main Street, and when a car drives by the window shakes, which is one of the reasons I leave it open most of the time. That and the fact I can hope for some sort of breeze to stir the dead, hot air around. The place is over a used book store called MARTHA'S BOOKS, and Martha is an all right lady if you like them mean. She's grumpy, about five hundred years old, weighs two-fifty when she's at her wrestling weight, wears men's clothing and has a bad leg and a faint black mustache to match the black wool ski cap she wears summer or winter, on account of her head is as bald as a river stone. I figure the cap is a funny sort of vanity, considering she doesn't do anything to get rid of that mustache. Still, she always does her nails in pink polish and she smokes those long feminine cigarettes that some women like, maybe thinking if the weeds look elegant enough they won't give them cancer.

Another thing about Martha, is with that bad leg she has a limp, and she helps that along with a gold putter she uses as a cane, putter side up for a handle. See her coming down the street, which isn't often, you got to think there's not much you could add to make her any more gaudy, unless it's an assful of bright tail feathers and maybe some guys to follow her playing percussion instruments.

I liked to go down to Martha's from time to time and browse the books, and if I had a little spare change, I'd try to actually buy something now and then, or get something for Jasmine. I was especially fond of detective books, and Jasmine, bless her little heart, liked Harlequin Romances. She'd read them four or five a weekend when she wasn't dating boys, and since she was dating quite regularly now, she'd cut back mostly to one or two Harlequins a weekend. Still, that was too many. I kept hoping she'd outgrow it. The romance novels and the dates. I was scared to death she'd fall in love with some cowboy with a cheek full of snuff and end up ironing Western shirts and wiping baby asses before she was old enough to vote.

Anyway, after I didn't find any jobs and nobody died and left me any money, I went home and brooded, then went downstairs to Martha's to look for a book.

Jasmine had made out a list of the titles she was looking to collect, and I took the list with me just in case I came across something she needed. I thought if I did, I might buy it and get her a detective book too, or something like that, give it to her with the romance and maybe she'd read it. I'd done that several times, and so far, to the best of my knowledge, she hadn't read any of the non-Romance novels. The others might as well have been used to level a vibrating refrigerator, but I kept on trying.

The stairs went down from my place and out into the street, and at the bottom, to the left of them, was Martha's. The store was in front and she lived in back. During business hours in the summer the door was always open since Martha wouldn't have put air-conditioning in there if half the store had been a meat locker hung with prize beef. She was too cheap for that. She liked her mustache sweat-beaded, her bald head pink beneath her cap. The place smelled of books and faintly of boiled cabbage, or maybe that was some soured clothing somewhere. The two smells have always seemed a lot alike to me. It's the only place I know hotter and filthier than my apartment, but it does have the books. Lots of them.

I went in, and there on the wall was a flyer for a circus at three o'clock that day. Martha had this old post board just inside the door, and she'd let people pin up flyers if they wanted, and sometimes she'd leave them there a whole day before she tore them down and wrote out the day's receipts on the back of them with a stubby, tongue-licked pencil. I think that's the only reason she had the post board and let people put up flyers, so she'd have scratch paper.

The flyer was for a circus called THE JIM DANDY THREE RING CIRCUS, and that should have clued me, but it didn't. Truth is, I've never liked circuses. They depress me. Something about the animals and the people who work there strike me as desperate as if they're living on the edge of a cliff and the cliff is about to break off. But I saw this flyer and I thought of Jasmine.

When she was little she loved circuses. Her mother and I used to take her, and I remembered the whole thing rather fondly. Jasmine would laugh so hard at the clowns you had to tell her to shut up, and she'd put her hands over her eyes and peek through her fingers at the wild animal acts.

Back then, things were pretty good, and I think her mother even liked me, and truth to tell, I thought I was a pretty good guy myself. I thought I had the world by the tail. It took me a few years to realize the closest I was to having the world by the tail was being a dingle berry on one of its ass hairs. These days, I felt like the most worthless sonofabitch that had ever squatted to shit over a pair of shoes. I guess it isn't hip or politically correct, but to me, a man without a job is like a man without balls.

Thinking about my problems also added to me wanting to go to the circus. Not only would I get a chance to be with Jasmine, it would help me get my mind off my troubles.

I got out my wallet and opened it and saw a few sad bills in there, but it looked to me that I had enough for the circus, and maybe I could even spring for dinner afterwards, if Jasmine was in the mood for a hot dog and a soda pop. She wanted anything more than that, she had to buy me dinner, and I'd let her, since the money came from her mother, my darling ex-wife, Connie—may she grow like an onion with her head in the ground.

Mommy Dearest didn't seem to be shy of the bucks these days on account of she was letting old Gerald the Oil Man drop his drill down her oil shaft on a nightly basis.

Not that I'm bitter about it or anything. Him banging my ex-wife and being built like Tarzan and not losing any of his hair at the age of forty didn't bother me a bit.

I put my wallet away and turned and saw Martha behind the counter looking at me. She twisted on the stool and said, "Got a job yet?"

I just love a small town. You fart and everyone looks in your direction and starts fanning.

"No, not yet," I said.

"You looking for some kind of a career?"

"I'm looking for work."

"Any kind of work?"

"Right now, yes. You got something for me?"

"Naw. Can't pay my rent as it is."

"You're just curious, then?"

"Yeah. You want to go to that circus?"

"I don't know. Maybe. Is this a trick question too?"

"Guy put up the flyer gave me a couple tickets for letting him have the space on the board there. I'd give them to you for stacking some books. I don't really want to do it."

"Stack the books or give me the tickets?"

"Neither one. But you stack them Harlequins for me, I'll give you the tickets."

I looked at my wrist where my watch used to be before I pawned it. "You got the time?"

She looked at her watch. "Two o'clock."

"I like the deal," I said, "but the circus starts at three and I wanted to take my daughter."

Martha shook out one of her delicate little cigarettes and lit it, studied me. It made me feel funny. Like I was a shit smear on a laboratory slide. Most I'd ever talked to her before was when I asked where the new detective novels were and she grumped around and finally told me, as if it was a secret she'd rather have kept.

"Tell you what," Martha said, "I'll give you the tickets now, and you come back tomorrow morning and put up the books for me."

"That's nice of you," I said.

"Not really. I know where you live, and you don't come put up my romance novels tomorrow, I'll hunt you down and kill you."

I looked for a smile, but I didn't see any.

"That's one way to do business," I said.

"The only way. Here." She opened a drawer and pulled out the tickets and I went over and took them. "By the way, what's your name, boy? See you in here all the time, but don't know your name."

Boy? Was she talking to me?

"Plebin Cook," I said. "And I've always assumed you're Martha."

"Martha ain't much of a name, but it beats Plebin. Plebin's awful. I was named that I'd get it changed. Call yourself most anything and it'd be better than Plebin."

"I'll tell my poor, old, grey-haired mother what you said."

"You must have been an accident and that's why she named you that. You got an older brother or sister?"

"A brother."

"How much older?"

Earning these tickets was getting to be painful. "Sixteen years."

"What's his name?"

"Jim."

"There you are. You were an accident. Jim's a normal name. Her naming you Plebin is unconscious revenge. I read about stuff like that in one of those psychology books came in. Called KNOW WHY THINGS HAPPEN TO YOU. You ought to read it. Thing it'd tell you is to get your named changed to something normal. Right name will give you a whole nuther outlook about yourself."

I had a vision of shoving those circus tickets down her throat, but I restrained myself for Jasmine's sake. "No joke? Well, I'll see you tomorrow."

"Eight o'clock sharp. Go stacking 'em after nine, gets so hot in here you'll faint. A Yankee visiting some relatives came in here and did just that. Found him about closing time over there by the historicals and the Gothic Romances. Had to call an ambulance to come get him. Got out of here with one of my Gothics clutched in his hand. Didn't pay me a cent for it."

"And people think a job like this is pretty easy."

"They just don't know," Martha said.

I said thanks and good-bye and started to turn away.

"Hey," Martha said. "You decide to get your name changed, they'll do stuff like that for you over at the court house."

"I'll keep that in mind," I said.

I didn't want any more of Martha, so I went over to the drug store and used the pay phone there and called Jasmine. Her mother answered.

"Hi, Connie," I said.

"Get a job yet?"

"No," I said. "But I'm closing in on some prospects."

"Bet you are. What do you want?"

"Jasmine in?"

"You want to talk to her?"

No, I thought. Just ask for the hell of it. But I said, "If I may." The phone clattered on something hard, a little more violently than necessary, I thought. A moment later Jasmine came on the line. "Daddy."

"Hi, Baby Darling. Want to go to the circus?"

"The circus?"

"The Jim Dandy Circus is in town, and I've got tickets."

"Yeah. Really." She sounded as if I'd asked her if she wanted to have her teeth cleaned.

"You used to like the circuses."

"When I was ten."

"That was just seven years ago."

"That's a long time."

"Only when you're seventeen. Want to go or not? I'll even spring for a hot dog."

"You know what they make hot dogs out of?"

"I try not to think about it. I figure I get some chili on it, whatever's in the dog dies."

"Guess you want me to come by and get you?"

"That would be nice. Circus starts at three. That's less than an hour away."

"All right, but Daddy?"

"Yeah."

"Don't call me Baby Darling in public. Someone could hear."

"We can't have that."

"Really, Daddy. I'm getting to be a woman now. It's . . . I don't know . . . kind of . . ."

"Hokey?"

"That's it."

"Gottcha."

The circus was not under the big top, but was inside the Mud Creek Exhibition center, which Mud Creek needs about as much as I need a second dick. I don't use the first one as it is. Oh, I pee out of it, but you know what I mean.

The circus was weak from the start, but Jasmine seemed to have a pretty good time, even if the performing bears were so goddamned old I thought we were going to have to go down there and help them out of their cages. The tiger act was scary, because it looked as if the tigers were definitely in control, but the overweight Ringmaster got out alive, and the elephants came on, so old and wrinkled they looked like drunks in baggy pants. That was the best of it. After that, the dog act, conducted by Waldo the Great, got out of hand, and his performing poodles went X-rated, and the real doo-doo hit the fan.

Idiot trainer had apparently put one of the bitches to work while she was in heat, and in response, the male dogs jumped her and started poking, the biggest male finally winning the honors and the other five running about as if their brains had rolled out of their ears.

Waldo the Great went a little nuts and started kicking the

fornicating dogs, but they wouldn't let up. The male dog kept his goober in the slot even when Waldo's kicks made his hind legs leave the ground. He didn't even yip.

I heard a kid behind us say, "Mommy, what are the puppies doing?"

And the Mommy, not missing a beat, said, "They're doing a trick, dear."

Children were screaming. Waldo began kicking the remaining dogs indiscriminately, and they darted for cover. Members of the circus rushed Waldo the Great. There were disappointed and injured dogs hunching and yipping all over the place. Waldo went back to the horny male and tried once more to discourage him. He really put the boot to him, but the ole boy really hung in there. I was kind of proud of him. One of the other dogs, innocent, except for confusion, and a gyrating ass and a dick like a rolled-back lipstick tube, made an error in geography and humped air past Waldo and got a kick in the ass for it.

He sailed way up and into the bleachers, went so high his fleas should have served cocktails and dinner on him. Came down like a bomb, hit between a crack in the bleachers with a yip. I didn't see him come out from under there. He didn't yip again.

The little boy behind me said, "Is that a trick too?"

"Yes," Mommy said. "It doesn't hurt him. He knows how to land."

I certainly hoped so.

Not everyone took it as casually as Mommy. Some dog lovers came out of the bleachers and there was a fight. Couple of cowboys started trying to do to Waldo what he had done to the poodles.

Meanwhile, back at the ranch, so to speak, the two amorous mutts were still at it, the male laying pipe like there was no tomorrow.

Yes sir, a pleasant afternoon trip to the circus with my

daughter. Another debacle. It was merely typical of the luck I had been experiencing. Even a free ticket to the circus could turn to shit.

Jasmine and I left while a cowboy down from the bleachers was using Waldo the Great as a punching bag. One of the ungrateful poodles was biting the cowboy on the boot.

Me and Jasmine didn't have hot dogs. We ended up at a Mexican place, and Jasmine paid for it. Halfway through the meal Jasmine looked up at me and frowned.

"Daddy, I can always count on you for a good time."

"Hey," I said, "what were you expecting for free tickets? Goddamn Ringling Brothers?"

"Really, Daddy. I enjoyed it. Weirdness follows you around. At Mom's there isn't anything to do but watch television, and Mom and Gerald always go to bed about nine o'clock, so they're no fun."

"I guess not," I said, thinking nine o'clock was awful early to be sleepy. I hoped the sonofabitch gave her the clap.

After dinner, Jasmine dropped me off and next morning I went down to Martha's and she grunted at me and showed me the Harlequins and where they needed to go, in alphabetical order, so I started placing them. After about an hour of that, it got hot and I had to stop and talk Martha into letting me go over to the drug store and buy a Coke.

When I came back with it, there was a guy in there with a box of Harlequin romances. He was tall and lean and not bad looking, except that he had one of those little pencil mustaches that look as if he'd missed a spot shaving or had a stain line from sipping chocolate milk. Except for a black eye, his face was oddly unlined, as if little that happened to him in life found representation there. I thought he looked familiar. A moment later, it came to me. He was the guy at the circus with the performing dogs. I hadn't recognized him without his gold lamé tights. I could picture him clearly now, his foot up in the air, a poodle being launched from it. Waldo the Great.

He had a box of books on the desk in front of Martha. All Harlequin Romances. He reached out and ran his fingers over the spines. "I really hate to get rid of these," he was saying to Martha, and his voice was as sweet as a cooing turtle dove. "Really hate it, but see, I'm currently unemployed and extra finances, even of a small nature, are needed, and considering all the books I read, well, they're outgrowing my trailer. I tell you, it hurts me to dispense with these. Just seeing them on my shelves cheers me . . . Oh, I take these books so to heart. If life could be like these, oh what a life that would be. But somebody always messes it up." He touched the books. "True love. Romance. Happy endings. Oh, it should be that way, you know. We live such a miserable existence. We—"

"Hey," Martha said. "Actually, I don't give a shit why you want to get rid of them. And if life was like a Harlequin Romance, I'd put a gun in my mouth. You want to sell this crap, or not?"

Martha always tries to endear herself to her customers. I reckon she's got a trust fund somewhere and her mission on earth is to make as many people miserable as possible. Still, that seemed blunt even for her.

"Well, now," Waldo said. "I was merely expressing a heartfelt opinion. Nothing more. I could take my trade elsewhere."

"No skin off my rose red ass," Martha said. "You want, that man over there will help you carry this shit back out to the car."

He looked at me. I blushed, nodded, drank more of my Coke.

He looked back at Martha. "Very well. I'll sell them to you, but only because I'm pressed to rid myself of them.

Otherwise, I wouldn't take twice what you want to give for them.''

"For you, Mister Asshole," Martha said, "just for you, I'll give you half of what I normally offer. Take it or leave it.''

Waldo, Mr. Asshole, paused for a moment, studying Martha. I could see the side of his face, and just below his blackened eye there was a twitch, just once, then his face was smooth again.

"All right, let's conduct our business and get it over with," he said.

Martha counted the books, opened the cash register and gave Waldo a handful of bills. "Against my better judgment, there's the whole price.''

"What in the world did I ever do to you?" Waldo the Great, alias, Mr. Asshole, said. He almost looked really hurt. It was hard to tell. I'd never seen a face like that. So smooth. So expressionless. It was disconcerting.

"You breathe," Martha said, "that's enough of an offense." With that, Waldo, Mr. Asshole, went out of the store, head up, back straight.

"Friend of yours?" I asked.

"Yeah," Martha said. "Me and him are fuckin'."

"I thought the two of you were pretty warm."

"I don't know. I really can't believe it happened like that.''

"You weren't as sweet as usual."

"Can't explain it. One of those things. Ever had that happen? Meet someone right off, and you just don't like them, and you don't know why."

"I always just shoot them. Saves a lot of breath."

She ignored me. "Like it's chemistry or something. That guy came in here, it was like someone drove by and tossed a rattlesnake through the door. I didn't like him on sight. Sometimes I think that there's certain people that are predators, and the rest of us, we pick up on it, even if it isn't obvious through their actions, and we react to it. And maybe I'm an asshole.''

"That's a possibility," I said. "You being an asshole, I mean. But I got to tell you, I don't like him much either. Kind of makes my skin crawl, that unlined face and all.''

I told her about the circus and the dogs.

"That doesn't surprise me any," Martha said. "I mean, anyone can lose their cool. I've kicked a dog in my time—''

"I find that hard to believe."

"—but I tell you, that guy hasn't got all the corn on his cob. I can sense it. Here, put these up. Earn your goddamn circus tickets.''

I finished off the Coke, got the box of Harlequins Waldo had brought in, took them over to the romance section and put them on the floor.

I pulled one out to look at the author's name, and something fell out of the book. It was a folded piece of paper. I picked it up and unfolded it. It was a magazine fold-out of a naked woman, sort you see in the cheaper tits and ass magazines. She had breasts just a little smaller than watermelons and she was grabbing her ankles, holding her legs in a spread eagle position, as if waiting for some unsuspecting traveler to fall in. There were thick black paint lines slashed at the neck, torso, elbows, wrist, waist, knees, and ankles. The eyes had been blackened with a marker so that they looked like nothing more than enormous skull sockets. A circle had been drawn around her vagina and there was a big black dot dead center of it, like a bull's-eye. I turned it over. On the back over the printing there was writing in black with a firm hand: Nothing really hooks together. Life lacks romance.

Looking at the photograph and those lines made me feel peculiar. I refolded the fold-out and started to replace it inside the book, then I thought maybe I'd throw it in the trash, but finally decided to keep it out of curiosity.

I shoved it into my back pocket and finished putting up the books, then got ready to leave. As I was going, Martha said, "You want a job here putting up books I'll take you on half a day five days a week. Monday through Friday. Saves some wear on my bad leg. I can pay you a little. Won't be much, but I don't figure you're worth much to me."

"That's a sweet offer, Martha, but I don't know."

"You say you want work."

"I do, but half a day isn't enough."

"More than you're working now, and I'll pay in cash. No taxes, no bullshit with the employment office."

"All right," I said. "You got a deal."

"Start tomorrow."

I was lying naked on the bed with just the night light on reading a hard-boiled mystery novel. The window was open as always and there was actually a pretty nice breeze blowing in. I felt like I used to when I was twelve and staying up late and reading with a flashlight under the covers and a cool spring wind was blowing in through the window screen, and Mom and Dad were in the next room and I was loved and protected and was going to live forever. Pleasant.

There was a knock at the door.

That figured.

I got up and pulled on my pajama bottoms and put on a robe and went to the door. It was Jasmine. She had her long, dark hair tied back in a pony tail and she was wearing jeans and a shirt buttoned up wrong. She had a suitcase in her hand.

"Connie again?"

"Her and that man," Jasmine said as she came inside. "I hate them."

"You don't hate your mother. She's an asshole, but you don't hate her."

"You hate her."

"That's different."

"Can I stay here for awhile?"

"Sure. There's almost enough room for me, so I'm sure you'll find it cozy."

"You're not glad to see me?"

"I'm glad to see you. I'm always glad to see you. But this won't work out. Look how small this place is. Besides, you've done this before. Couple times. You come here, eat all my cereal, start missing your comforts, and then you go home."

"Not this time."

"All right. Not this time. Hungry?"

"I really don't want any cereal."

"I actually have some lunch meat this time. It's not quite green."

"Sounds yummy."

I made a couple of sandwiches and poured us some slightly tainted milk and we talked a moment, then Jasmine saw the fold-out on the dresser and picked it up. I had pulled it from my pocket when I got home and tossed it there.

She opened it up and looked at it, then smiled at me. It was the same smile her mother used when she was turning on the charm, or was about to make me feel small enough to wear doll clothes.

"Daddy, dear!"

"I found it."

"Say you did?"

"Cut it out. It was in one of the books I was putting up today. I thought it was weird and I stuck it in my back pocket. I should have thrown it away."

Jasmine smiled at me, examined the fold-out closely. "Daddy, do men like women like this? That big, I mean?"

"Some do. Yes."

"Do you?"

"Of course not."

"What are these lines?"

"I don't know exactly, but that's what I thought was weird. It got my mind working overtime."

"You mean like the 'What If' game?"

The "What If" game was something Jasmine and I had made up when she was little, and had never really quit playing, though our opportunities to play it had decreased sharply over the last couple of years. It grew out of my thinking I was going to be a writer. I'd see something and I'd extrapolate. An example was an old car I saw once where someone had finger-written in the dust on the trunk lid: THERE'S A BODY IN THE TRUNK.

Well, I thought about that and tried to make a story of it. Say there was a body in the trunk. How did it get there? Is the woman driving the car aware it's there? Did she commit the murder? That sort of thing. Then I'd try to write a story. After fifty or so stories, and three times that many rejects, I gave up writing them, and Jasmine and I started kicking ideas like that back and forth, for fun. That way I could still feed my imagination, but I could quit kidding myself that I could write. Also, Jasmine got a kick out of it.

"Let's play, Daddy?"

"All right. I'll start. I saw those slashes on that fold-out, and I got to thinking, why are these lines drawn?"

"Because they look like cuts," Jasmine said. "You know, like a chart for how to butcher meat."

"That's what I thought. Then I thought, it's just a picture, and it could have been marked up without any real motive. Absentminded doodling. Or it could have been done by someone who didn't like women, and this was sort of an imaginary revenge. Turning women into meat in his mind. Dehumanizing them."

"Or it could be representative of what he's actually done or plans to do. Wow! Maybe we've got a real mystery here."

"My last real mystery was what finished your mom and I off."

That was the body in the trunk business. I didn't tell it all before. I got so into that scenario I called a friend of mine, Sam, down at the cop shop and got him geared up about there being a body in the trunk of a car. I told it good, with details I'd made up and didn't even know I'd made up. I really get into this stuff. The real and the unreal get a little hard for me to tell apart. Or it used to be that way. Not anymore.

Bottom line is Sam pursued the matter, and the only thing in the trunk was a spare tire. Sam was a little unhappy with me. The cop shop was a little unhappy with him. My wife, finally tired of my make-believe, kicked me out and went for the oil man. He didn't make up stories. He made money and had all his hair and was probably hung like a water buffalo.

"But say we knew the guy who marked this picture, Daddy. And say we started watching him, just to see—"

"We do know him. Kind of."

I told her about Waldo the Great and his books and Martha's reaction.

"That's even weirder," Jasmine said. "This bookstore lady—"

"Martha."

"—does she seem like a good judge of character?"

"She hates just about everybody, I think."

"Well, for 'What If's' sake, say she is a good judge of character. And this guy really is nuts. And he's done this kind of thing to a fold-out because . . . say . . . say . . ."

"He wants life to be like a Harlequin Romance. Only it

isn't. Women don't always fit his image of what they should be—like the women in the books he reads.''

"Oh, that's good, Daddy. Really. He's gone nuts, not because of violent films and movies, but because of a misguided view about romance. I love it.''

"Makes as much sense as a guy saying he axed a family because he saw a horror movie or read a horror novel. There's got to be more to it than that, of course. Rotten childhood, genetic makeup. Most people who see or read horror novels, romance novels, whatever, get their thrills vicariously. It's a catharsis. But in the same way a horror movie or book might set someone off who's already messed up, someone wound up and ready to spring, the Harlequins do it for our man. He has so little idea what real life is like, he expects it to be like the Harlequins, or desperately wants it to be that way, and when it isn't, his frustrations build, and—''

"He kills women, cuts them up, disposes of their bodies. It's delicious. Really delicious.''

"It's silly. There's a sleeping bag in the closet. Get it out when you get sleepy. Me, I'm going to go to bed. I got a part-time job downstairs at Martha's, and I start tomorrow.''

"That's great, Daddy. Mom said you'd never find a job.''

On that note, I went to bed.

Next morning I went down to Martha's and started to work. She had a storeroom full of books. Some of them were stuck together with age, and some were full of worms. Being a fanatic book lover, it hurt me, but I got rid of the bad ones in the dumpster out back, then loaded some boxes of good condition books on a hand truck and wheeled them out and began putting them up in alphabetical order in their proper sections.

About nine that morning, Jasmine came down and I heard her say something to Martha, then she came around the

corner of the detective section and smiled at me. She looked
so much like her mother it hurt me. She had her hair pulled
back and tied at her neck and she was starting to sweat. She
wore white shorts, cut a little too short if you ask me, and a
loose red T-shirt and sandals. She was carrying a yellow pad
with a pencil.

"What you doing?" I asked.

"Figuring out what Waldo the Great's up to. I been
working on it ever since I got up. I got lots of notes here."

"What'd you have for breakfast?"

"Same as you, I bet. A Coke."

"Right. It's important we pay attention to nutrition, Baby
Darling."

"You want to hear about Waldo or not?"

"Yeah, tell me, what's he up to?"

"He's looking for a job."

"Because he got fired for the dog kicking business?"

"Yeah. So, he's staying in the trailer park here, and he's
looking for a job. Or maybe he's got some savings and he's
just hanging out for a while before he moves on. Let's just
say all that for 'What If's' sake."

"All right, now what?"

"Just for fun, to play the game all the way, let's go out to
the trailer park and see if he's living there. If he is, we ought
to be able to find him. He's got all these dogs, so there
should be some signs of them, don't you think?"

"Wait a minute. You're not planning on checking?"

"Just for the 'What If' game."

"Like I said, he could have moved on."

"That's what we'll find out. Later, we can go over to the
trailer park and look around, play detective."

"That's carrying it too far."

"Why? It's just a game. We don't have to bother him."

"I don't know. I don't think so."

"Why not?" It was Martha. She came around the corner

of the bookshelves leaning on her golf putter. "It's just a game."

"Aren't you supposed to be counting your money, or something?" I said to Martha. "Kill some of those roaches in your storeroom. That club would be just the tool for it."

"I couldn't help but overhear you because I was leaning against the other side of the bookshelf listening," Martha said.

"That'll do it," I said, and shelved a Mickey Spillane.

"We've spoke, but I don't think we've actually met," Jasmine said to Martha. "I'm his daughter."

"Tough to admit, I'm sure," Martha said.

Jasmine and Martha smiled at each other and shook hands.

"Why don't we go over there tonight?" Martha said. "I need something to do."

"To the trailer park?" I asked.

"Of course," Martha said.

"Not likely," I said. "I've had it with the detective business, imaginary or otherwise. It'll be a cold day in hell when I have anything else to do with it, in any manner, shape or form. And you can take that to the bank."

That night, presumably an example of a cold day in hell, around nine thirty, we drove over to the only trailer park in Mud Creek and looked around.

Waldo hadn't moved on. Being astute detectives, we found his trailer right away. It was bright blue and there was red lettering on the side that read: WALDO THE GREAT AND HIS MAGNIFICENT CANINES. The trailer was next to a big pickup with a trailer hitch and there were lights on in the trailer.

We were in Martha's old Dodge van, and we drove by Waldo's and around the loop in the park and out of there. Martha went a short distance, turned down a hard clay road

that wound along the side of the creek and through a patch
of woods and ended up at the rear of the trailer park, about
even with Waldo's trailer. It was a bit of distance away, but
you could see his trailer through the branches of the trees
that surrounded the park. Martha parked on the side of the
road and spoke to Jasmine. "Honey, hand me them binoculars out of the glove box."

Jasmine did just that.

"These suckers are infra-red," Martha said. "You can
see a mole on a gnat's ass with one of these dead of night
during a blizzard."

"And why in the world would you have a pair?" I asked.

"I used to do a little surveillance for a private investigation agency in Houston. I sort of borrowed these when I left.
You know, boss I had hadn't been such a dick, I'd have
stayed with that job. I was born to it."

"Sounds exciting," Jasmine said.

"It beats smelling book dust, I'll tell you that." Martha
rolled down her window and put the glasses on her face and
pointed them at Waldo's trailer.

"He's at the window," she said.

"This has gone far enough," I said. "We're not supposed to be doing this. It's an invasion of privacy."

"Settle down. He ain't got his pecker out or nothing,"
Martha said. "Wish he did, though. He's an asshole, but he
ain't bad looking. I wonder what kind of rod he's got on
him?"

I looked at Jasmine. She looked a little stunned. "Listen
here," I said. "My daughter's here."

"No shit," Martha said. "Listen, you stuffy old fart.
She's grown up enough to know a man's got a hooter on
him and what it looks like."

Jasmine's face was split by a weak smile. "Well, I know
what they are, of course."

"All right, we're all versed in biology," I said. "Let's go. I've got a good book waiting at home."

"Hold the goddamn phone," Martha said. "He's coming out of the trailer."

I looked, and I could see Waldo's shape framed in the trailer's doorway. One of the poodles ran up behind him and he back-kicked it inside without even looking, went down the metal steps and closed and locked the trailer, got in his pickup and drove away.

"He's off," Martha said.

"Yeah. Probably to a fried chicken place," I said.

Martha lowered the binoculars and looked over her seat at me. "Would you quit fucking up the game? 'What If' is going on here."

"Yeah, Daddy," Jasmine said. "We're playing 'What If'."

Martha cranked the van and followed the clay road as it curved around the park and out into the street. She went right. A moment later, we saw the back of Waldo's pickup. He had an arm hanging out the window and a cigarette was between his fingers and sparks were flaring off of it and flickering into the night.

"Smokey Bear'd come down on his ass like a ton of bricks, he seen that," Martha said.

We followed him to the end of the street and out onto the main drag, such as it is in Mud Creek. He pulled into a fried chicken joint.

"See," I said.

"Even murderers have to eat," Martha said, and she drove on by.

My plan was to end the business there, but it didn't work that way. I pulled out of it and let them stay with it. All that week Martha and Jasmine played 'What If'. They pinned up the foldout in my apartment and they wrote out scenarios for who Waldo was and what he'd done, and so on. They drove out to his place at night and discovered he kept weird hours, went out at all times of the night. They discovered he let the poodles out for bathroom breaks twice a night and that there was one less than there had been during the circus act. I guess Mommy had been wrong when she told her kid the poodle knew how to land.

It was kind of odd seeing Jasmine and Martha become friends like that. Martha had struck me as having all the imagination of a fence post, but under that rough exterior and that loud mouth was a rough exterior and a loud mouth with an imagination.

I also suspicioned that she had lied about not being able to pay her rent. The store didn't make that much, but she always seemed to have money. As far as the store went, it got so I was running it by myself, full-time, not only putting up books, but waiting on customers and closing up at night. Martha paid me well enough for it, however, so I didn't complain, but when she and Jasmine would come down from my place talking about their ''killer'', etc., I felt a little jealous. Jasmine had moved in with me, and now that I had my daughter back, she spent all her time with a bald-headed, mustached lady who was her father's boss.

Worse, Connie had been on my case about Jasmine and how my only daughter was living in a shit hole and being exposed to bad elements. The worst being me, of course. She came by the apartment a couple of times to tell me about it and to try and get Jasmine to go home.

I told her Jasmine was free to go home anytime she chose, and Jasmine explained that she had no intention of going home. She liked her sleeping bag and Daddy let her have Coke for breakfast. I sort of wish she hadn't mentioned the Coke part. She'd only had that for breakfast one morning, but she knew it'd get her mother's goat, and it had. Only thing was, now Connie could hang another sword over my head. Failure to provide proper nutrition for my only child.

Anyway, I was working in the store one day—well, working on reading a detective novel—when Martha and Jasmine came in.

"Get your goddamn feet off my desk," Martha said.

"Glad to see you," I said, lowering my feet and putting a marker in the book.

"Get off my stool," Martha said. "Quit reading that damn book and put some up."

I got off the stool. "You two have a pleasant day, Massah Martha?"

"Eat shit, Plebin," Martha said, leaning her golf club against the counter and mounting her stool.

"Daddy, Martha and I have been snooping. Listen what we got. Martha had this idea to go over to the newspaper office in LaBorde and look at back issues—"

"LaBorde?" I said.

"Bigger town. Bigger paper," Martha said, sticking one of her dainty cigarettes into her mouth and lighting it.

"We went through some older papers," Jasmine said, "and since LaBorde covers a lot of the small towns around here, we found ads for the Jim Dandy Circus in several of them, and we were able to pinpoint on a map the route of the circus up to Mud Creek, and the latest paper showed Marvel Creek to be the next stop, and—"

"Slow down," I said. "What's the circus got to do with your so-called investigation?"

"You look at the papers and read about the towns where the circus showed up," Martha said, "and there's in every one of them something about a missing woman, or young girl. In a couple cases, bodies have been found. Sometimes they were found a week or so after the circus came to town, but most of the news articles indicate the missing women disappeared at the time of the circus."

"Of course, we determined this, not the papers," Jasmine said. "We made the connection between the circus and the bodies."

"In the case of the bodies, both were found after the circus passed through," Martha said, "but from the estimated times of death the papers gave, we've been able to figure they were killed about the time the circus was in town. And my guess is those missing women are dead too, and by the same hand."

"Waldo's?" I said.

"That's right," Martha said.

I considered all that.

Jasmine said, "Pretty coincidental, don't you think?"

"Well, yeah," I said, "but that doesn't mean—"

"And the two bodies had been mutilated," Martha said. She leaned against the counter and reached into her shirt pocket and pulled out the fold-out I had found. She smoothed it out on the counter top. "Body parts were missing. And I bet they were cut up, just like this fold-out is marked. As for the missing body parts, eyes and pussies, I figure. Those are the parts he has circled and blacked out."

"Watch your language," I said to Martha.

No one seemed to take much note of me.

"The bodies were found in the town's local dump," Jasmine said.

"It's curious," I admitted, "but still, to accuse a man of murder on the basis of circumstantial evidence."

"One more thing," Martha said. "Both bodies had traces of black paint on them. Like it had been used to mark the areas the killer wanted to cut, and I presume, did cut. That's certainly a lot of goddamn circumstantial evidence, isn't it?"

"Enough that we're going to keep an eye on Waldo," Jasmine said.

* * *

I must admit right now that I didn't think even then, after what I had been told, there was anything to this Waldo the Great as murderer. It struck me that murders and disappearances happen all the time, and that if one were to look through the LaBorde paper carefully, it would be possible to discover there had been many of both, especially disappearances, before and after the arrival of the circus. I mean that paper covered a lot of small towns and communities, and LaBorde was a fairly large town itself. A small city actually. Most of the disappearances would turn out to be nothing more than someone leaving on a trip for a few days without telling anyone, and most of the murders would be committed by a friend or relative of the victim and would have nothing to do with the circus or marked up fold-outs.

Of course, the fact that the two discovered bodies had been mutilated gave me pause, but not enough to go to the law about it. That was just the sort of half-baked idea that had gotten my ass in a crack earlier.

Still, that night, I went with Martha and Jasmine out to the trailer park.

It was cloudy that night and jags of lightning made occasional cuts through the cloud cover and thunder rumbled and light drops of rain fell on the windshield of Martha's van.

We drove out to the road behind the park about dark, peeked out the windows and through the gaps in the trees. The handful of pole lights in the park were gauzy in the wet night and sad as dying fireflies. Their poor, damp rays fell against some of the trees—their branches waving in the wind like the fluttering hands of distressed lunatics—and forced the beads of rain on the branches to give up tiny rainbows. The rainbows rose up, misted outward a small distance, then once beyond the small circumference of light, their beauty was consumed by the night.

Martha got out her binoculars and Jasmine sat on the front passenger side with a note pad and pen, ready to record anything Martha told her to. They felt that the more documentation they had, the easier it would be to convince the police that Waldo was a murderer.

I was in the seat behind theirs, my legs stretched out and my back against the van, looking away from the trailer most of the time, wondering how I had let myself in on this. About midnight I began to feel both sleepy and silly. I unwrapped a candy bar and ate it.

"Would you quit that goddamn smacking back there," Martha said. "It makes me nervous."

"Pardon me all to hell," I said, and wadded up the wrapper noisily and tossed it on the floorboard.

"Daddy, would you quit?" Jasmine said.

"Now we got something," Martha said.

I sat up and turned around. There were no lights on in the trailers in the park except for Waldo's trailer; a dirty, orange glow shone behind one of his windows, like a fresh slice of smoked cheese. Other than that, there was only the pole lights, and they didn't offer much. Just those little rainbows made of bad light and rain. Without the binoculars there was little to observe in detail, because it was a pretty good distance from where we were to Waldo's trailer, but I could see him coming out of the door, holding it open, the whole pack of poodles following after.

Waldo bent down by the trailer and pulled a small shovel out from beneath it. The poodles wandered around and started doing their bathroom business. Waldo cupped his hands over a cigarette and lit it with a lighter and smoked while he noted the dogs' delivery spots. After a while he went about scooping up their messes with his shovel and making several trips to the dumpster to get rid of it.

Finished, he pushed the shovel beneath the trailer and smoked another cigarette and ground it hard beneath his heel and opened the door and called to the dogs. They bounded up the steps and into the trailer like it was one of their circus tricks. No poodle tried to fuck another poodle. Waldo didn't kick anybody. He went inside, and a moment later came out again, this time minus the poodles. He was carrying something. A box. He looked about carefully, then placed the box in the back of his pickup. He went back inside the trailer.

"Goddamn," Martha said. "There's a woman's leg in that box."

"Let me see," I said.

"You can't see it now," she said. "It's down in the bed of the truck."

She gave me the binoculars anyway, and I looked. She was right. I couldn't see what was in the bed of the truck. "He wouldn't just put a woman's leg in the back of his pickup," I said.

"Well, he did," Martha said.

"Oh God," Jasmine said, and she flicked on her pen light and glanced at her watch and started writing on her note pad, talking aloud as she did. "Twelve-o-five, Waldo put woman's leg in the bed of his truck. Oh, shit, who do you think it could be?"

"One could hope it's that goddamn bitch down at the county clerk's office," Martha said. "I been waiting for something to happen to her."

"Martha!" Jasmine said.

"Just kidding," Martha said. "Kinda."

I had the binoculars tight against my face as the trailer door opened again. I could see very well with the infra-red business. Waldo came out with another box. As he came down the steps, the box tilted slightly. It was open at the top and I could see very clearly what was in it.

"A woman's head," I said. My voice sounded small and childish.

"Jesus Christ," Martha said. "I didn't really, really, believe he was a murderer."

Waldo was back inside the trailer. A moment later he reappeared. Smaller boxes under each arm.

"Let me see," Jasmine said.

"No," I said. "You don't need to."

"But . . ." Jasmine began.

"Listen to your father," Martha said.

I handed the binoculars back to Martha. She didn't look through them. We didn't need to try and see what was in the other boxes. We knew. The rest of Waldo's victim.

Waldo unfolded a tarp in the back of his pickup and stretched it across the truck bed and fastened it at all corners, then got inside the cab and cranked the engine.

"Do we go to the police now?" Jasmine said.

"After we find out where he's taking the body," Martha said.

"You're right," I said. "Otherwise, if he's disposed of all the evidence, we've got nothing." I was thinking too of my record at the police station. Meaning, of course, more than my word would be needed to start an investigation.

Martha cranked the van and put on the park lights and began to ease along, giving Waldo the time he needed to get out of the trailer park and ahead of us.

"I've got a pretty good idea where he's going," Martha said. "Bet he scoped the place out first day he got to town."

"The dump," Jasmine said. "Place they found those other bodies."

We got to the street and saw Waldo was headed in the direction of the dump. Martha turned on the van's headlights after the pickup was down the road a bit, then eased out in pursuit. We laid back and let him get way ahead, and when we got out of town and he took the turnoff to the dump, we passed on by and turned down a farm-to-market road and parked as close as we could to a barbed wire fence.

We got out and climbed the fence and crossed a pasture and came to a rise and went up that and poked our heads over carefully and looked down on the dump.

There was smoke rising up in spots, where pounds of burning refuse had been covered at some point, and it filled the air with stink. The dump had been like that forever. As a little boy, my father would bring me out to the dump to toss our family garbage, and even in broad daylight, I thought the place spooky, a sort of poor boy, blue collar hell. My dad said there were fires out here that had never been put out, not by the weight of garbage and dirt, or by winter ice or spring's rain storms. Said no matter what was done to those fires, they still burned. Methane maybe. All the stuff in the dump heating up like compost, creating some kind of combustible chemical reaction.

Within the dump, bordered off by a wide layer of scraped earth, were two great oil derricks. They were working derricks too, and the great rocking horse pumps dipped down and rose up constantly, night or day, and it always struck me that this was a foolish place for a dump full of never dying fires to exist, next to two working oil wells. But the dump still stood and the derricks still worked oil. The city council had tried to have the old dump shut down, moved, but so far nothing had happened. They couldn't get those fires out completely, for one thing. I felt time was against the dump and the wells. Eventually, the piper, or in this case, the pipeline, had to be paid. Some day the fires in the dump would get out of hand and set the oil wells on fire and the explosion that would occur would send Mud Creek and its surrounding rivers and woodlands to some place north of Pluto.

At night, the place was even more eerie. Flames licking out from under the debris like tongues, the rain seeping to its source, making it hiss white smoke like dragon breath. The two old derricks stood tall against the night and lightning

wove a flickering crown of light around one of them and
went away. In that instant, the electrified top of the derrick
looked like Martian machinery. Inside the derricks, the still
working well pumps throbbed and kerchunked and dipped
their dark metal hammer heads, then lifted them again.
Down and up. Down and up. Taking with them on the drop
and the rise, rain-wet shadows and flickers of garbage fire.

Waldo's truck was parked beside the road, next to a
mound of garbage the height of a first-story roof. He had
peeled off the tarp and put it away and was unloading his
boxes from the truck, carrying them to a spot near one of the
oil derricks, arranging them neatly, as if he were being
graded on his work. When the boxes were all out, Waldo
stood with his back to us and watched one of the derrick's
pumps nod for a long time, as if the action of it amazed or
offended him.

After a time, he turned suddenly and kicked at one of the
boxes. The head in it popped up like a Mexican jumping
bean and fell back down inside. Waldo took a deep breath,
as if he were preparing to run a race, then got in his truck,
turned it around, and drove away.

"He didn't even bother to bury the pieces," Jasmine said,
and even in the bad light, I could see she was as white as
Frosty the Snowman.

"Probably wants it to be found," Martha said. "We
know where the corpse is now. We have evidence, and we
saw him dispose of the body ourselves. I think we can go to
the law now."

We drove back to town and called Sam from Martha's
book store. He answered the phone on the fifth ring. He
sounded like he had a sock in his mouth.

"What?"

"Plebin, Sam. I need your help."

"You in a ditch? Call a wrecker, man. I'm bushed."

"Not exactly. It's about murder."

"Ah, shit, Plebin. You some kind of fool, or what? We been through this. Call some nuthouse doctor or something. I need sleep. Day I put in today was bad enough, but I don't need you now and some story about murder. Lack of sleep gives me domestic problems."

"This one's different. I've got two witnesses. A body out at the dump. We saw it disposed of. A woman cut up in pieces, I kid you not. Guy named Waldo did it. He used to be with the circus. Directed a dog act."

"The circus?"

"That's right."

"And he has a dog act."

"Had. He cut up a woman and took her to the dump."

"Plebin?"

"Yes."

"I go out there, and there's no dead body, I could change that, supply one, mood I'm in. Understand?"

"Just meet us at the dump."

"Who's us?"

I told him, gave him some background on Waldo, explained what Martha and Jasmine found in the LaBorde newspapers, hung up, and me and my fellow sleuths drove back to the dump.

We waited outside the dump in Martha's van until Sam showed in his blue Ford. We waved at him and started the van and led him into the dump. We drove up to the spot near the derrick and got out. None of us went over to the boxes for a look. We didn't speak. We listened to the pumps doing their work inside the derricks. Kerchunk, kerchunk, kerchunk.

Sam pulled up behind us and got out. He was wearing blue jeans and tennis shoes and his pajama top. He looked at me and Jasmine and Martha. Fact is, he looked at Martha quite a while.

"You want maybe I should send you a picture, or something?" Martha said.

Sam didn't say anything. He looked away from Martha and said to me, "All right. Where's the body?"

"It's kind of here and there," I said, and pointed. "In those boxes. Start with the little one, there. There's her head."

Sam looked in the box, and I saw him jump a little. Then he went still, bent forward and pulled the woman's head out by the hair, held it up in front of him and looked at it. He spun and tossed it to me. Reflexively, I caught it, then dropped it. By the time it hit the ground I felt like a number one horse's ass.

It wasn't a human head. It was a mannequin head with a black paint mark covering the stump of the neck, which had been neatly sawed in two.

"Here, Jasmine," Sam said. "You take a leg," and he hoisted a mannequin leg out of another box and tossed it at her. She shrieked and dodged and it landed on the ground. "And you that's gonna send me a picture. You take an arm." He pulled a mannequin arm out of another box and tossed it at Martha, who swatted it out of the air with her putter cane.

He turned and kicked another of the boxes and sent a leg and an arm sailing into a heap of brush and old paint cans.

"Goddamn it, Plebin," he said. "You've done it again." He came over and stood in front of me. "Man, you're nuts. Absolutely nuts."

"Wasn't just Plebin," Martha said. "We all thought it. The guy brought this stuff out here is a weirdo. We've been watching him."

"You have?" Sam said. "Playing detective, huh? That's sweet. That's real sweet. Plebin, come here, will you?"

I went over and stood by him. He put an arm around my shoulders and walked me off from Jasmine and Martha. He whispered to me.

"Plebin. You're not learning, man. Not a bit. Not only are you fucking up your life, you're fucking up mine. Listen here. Me and the old lady, we're not doing so good, see."

"I'm sorry to hear it. Toni has always been so great."

"Yeah, well, you see, she's jealous. You know that."

"Oh yeah. Always has been."

"There you are. She's gotten worse too. And you see, I spend a lot of time away from the home. Out of the bed. Bad hours. You getting what I'm saying here?"

"Yeah."

He pulled me closer and patted my chest with his other hand. "Good. Not only is that bad, me spending those hours away from home and out of the bed at bedtime, but hey, I'm so bushed these days, I get ready to lay a little pipe, well, I got no lead in the pencil. Like a goddamn spaghetti, that's how it is. Know what I'm saying?"

"Least when you do get it hard, you get to lay pipe," I said.

"But I'm not laying it enough. It's because I don't get rest. But Toni, you know what she thinks? She thinks it's because I'm having a little extra-curricular activity. You know what I mean? Thinks I'm out banging hole like there's no tomorrow."

"Hey, I'm sorry, Sam, but . . ."

"So now I've got the rest problem again. I'm tired right now. I don't recover like I used to. I don't get eight hours of sack time, hey, I can't get it up. I have a bad day, which I do when I'm tired, I can't get it up. My shit comes out different, I can't get it up. I've gotten sensitive in my old age. Everything goes straight to my dick. Toni, she gets ready for me to do my duty, guess what?"

"You're too tired. You can't get it up."

"Bingo. The ole Johnson is like an empty sock. And when I can't get it up, what does Toni think?"

"You're fucking around?"

"That's right. And it's not bad enough I gotta be tired for legitimate reasons, but now I got to be tired because you and your daughter and Ma Frankenstein over there are seeing heads in boxes. Trailing some innocent bystander and trying to tie him in with murder when there's nobody been murdered. Know what I'm saying?"

"Sam, the guy looks the part. Acts it. There's been murders everywhere the circus goes . . ."

"Plebin, ole buddy. Hush your mouth, okay? Listen up tight. I'm going home now. I'm going back to bed. You wake me up again, I'll run over you with a truck. I don't have a truck, but I'll borrow one for the purpose. Got me?"

"Yeah."

"All right. Good night." He took his arm off my shoulder, walked back to his car and opened the door. He started to get inside, then straightened. He looked over the roof at me. "Come by and have dinner next week. Toni still makes a good chicken fried steak. Been a while since she's seen you."

"I'll keep it in mind. Give her my love."

"Yeah. And Plebin, don't call with any more murders, all right? You got a good imagination, but as a detective, you're the worst." He looked at Jasmine. "Jasmine, you stick with your mother." He got in his car, backed around and drove away.

I went over and stood with my fellow sleuths and looked down at the mannequin head. I picked it up by the hair and looked at it. "I think I'll have this mounted," I said. "Just to remind me what a jackass I am."

Back at the apartment I sat on the bed with the window open, the mannequin head on the pillow beside me. Jasmine sat in the dresser chair and Martha had one of my rickety kitchen chairs turned around backwards and she sat with her arms crossed on the back of it, sweat running out from under her wool cap, collecting in her mustache.

"I still think something funny is going on there," Jasmine said.

"Oh, shut up," I said.

"We know something funny is going on," Martha said.

"We means you two," I said. "Don't include me. I don't know anything except I've made a fool out of myself and Sam is having trouble with his sex life, or maybe what he told me was some kind of parable."

"Sex life," Jasmine said. "What did he tell you?"

"Forget," I said.

"That Sam is some sorry cop," Martha said. "He should have at least investigated Waldo. Guy who paints and cuts up mannequins isn't your everyday fella, I'd think. I bet he's painting and sawing them up because he hasn't picked a victim yet. It's his way of appeasing himself until he's chosen someone. Akin to masturbation instead of real sex."

"If we could see inside his trailer," Jasmine said, "I bet we'd find evidence of something more than mannequins. Evidence of past crimes maybe."

"I've had enough," I said. "And Jasmine, so have you. And Martha, if you're smart, so have you."

Martha got out one of her little cigarettes.

"Don't light that in here," I said.

She got out a small box of kitchen matches.

"I can't stand smoke," I said.

She pulled a match from the box and struck it on her pants leg and lit up, puffed, studied the ceiling.

"Put it out, Martha. This is my place."

She blew smoke at the ceiling. "I think Jasmine's right," she said. "If we could divert him. Get him out of the trailer so we could have a look inside, find some evidence, then maybe that small town idiot cop friend of yours would even be convinced.''

"Waldo's not going to keep a human head in there,'' I said.

"He might,'' Martha said. "It's been known to happen. Or maybe something a victim owned. Guys like that keep souvenirs of their murders. That way they can fantasize, relive it all.''

"We could watch his place tomorrow,'' Jasmine said, "then if he goes out, we could slip in and look around. We find something incriminating, something definite, there's a way to cue the police in on it, even one as stubborn and stupid as Sam.''

"I'm sure Waldo locks his doors,'' I said.

"That's no trouble,'' Martha said. "I can pick the lock on Heaven's door.''

"You're just a basket of fine skills,'' I said.

"I used to work for a repo company, years back,'' Martha said. "I learned to use lock jocks and keys and picks on car doors and garage doors. You name it, I can get in it, and in a matter of moments.''

"Listen, you two,'' I said, "leave it be. We don't know this guy's done anything, and if he is a murderer, you damn sure don't need to be snooping around there, or you may end up on the victim list. Let's get on with our lives.''

"Such as yours and mine is,'' Martha said. "What have I got to look forward to? Selling a few books? Meeting the right man? Me, a gargoyle with a golf club?''

"Martha, don't say that,'' Jasmine said.

"No, let's call a spade a spade here,'' Martha said. She snatched off her wool cap and showed us her bald head. I had seen a glimpse of it a time or two before I went to work there, when she was taking off and adjusting her cap or scratching her head, but this was the first time I'd seen it in all its sweaty, pink glory for more than a few moments.

"What's gonna pull a mate in for me? My glorious head of hair. I started losing it when I was in my twenties. No man would look twice at me. Besides that, I'm ugly and have a mustache."

"A mate isn't everything," I said.

"It's something," Martha said. "And I think about it. I won't kid you. But I know it isn't possible. I've been around, seen some things, had some interesting jobs. But I haven't really made any life for myself. Not so it feels like one. And you know what? After all these years, Jasmine and you are my only real friends, and in your case, Plebin, I don't know that amounts to much."

"Thanks," I said.

"You could get a wig," Jasmine said.

"I could have these whiskers removed," Martha said. "But I'd still be a blimp with a bum leg. No. There's nothing for me in the looks department. Not unless I could change bodies with some blond bimbo. Since that isn't going to happen, all I got is what I make out of life. Like this mystery. A real mystery, I think. And if Waldo is a murderer, do we let him go on to the next town and find a victim? Or for that matter, a victim here, before he leaves?

"We catch this guy. Prove he's responsible for murders, then we've actually done something important with our lives. There's more to my life than the book store. More to yours Plebin than a bad name and unemployment checks. And . . . well, in your case Jasmine, there is more to your life. You're beautiful, smart, and you're going places. But for all of us, wouldn't it be worthwhile to catch a killer?"

"If he is a killer," I said. "Maybe he just hates mannequins because they look better in their clothes than he does."

"Women's clothes?" Jasmine said.

"Maybe it's women's clothes he likes to wear," I said.

"Thing is, we could end up making fools of ourselves, spend some time in jail, even."

"I'll chance it," Jasmine said.

"No you won't," I said. "It's over for you, Jasmine. Martha can do what she wants. But you and me, we're out of it."

Martha left.

Jasmine got out her sleeping bag and unrolled it, went to the bathroom to brush her teeth. I tried to stay awake and await my turn in there, but couldn't. Too tired. I lay down on the bed, noted vaguely that rain had stopped pounding on the apartment roof, and I fell immediately asleep.

I awoke later that night, early morning really, to the smell of more on-coming rain, and when I rolled over I could see flashes of lightning in the west.

The west. The direction of the dump. It was as if a storm was originating there, moving toward the town.

Melodrama. I loved it.

I rolled over and turned my head to the end-table beside the bed, and when the lightning flashed I could see the mannequin head setting there, its face turned toward me, its strange, false eyes alight with the fire of the western lightning. The paint around the mannequin's neck appeared very damp in that light, like blood.

I threw my legs from beneath the covers and took hold of the head. The paint on its neck was wet in my hands. The humidity had caused it to run. I sat the head on the floor where I wouldn't have to look at it, got up to go to the bathroom and wash my hands.

Jasmine's sleeping bag was on the floor, but Jasmine wasn't in it. I went on to the bathroom, but she wasn't in there either. I turned on the light and washed my hands and felt a little weak. There was no place else to be in the apartment. I looked to see if she had taken her stuff and gone home, but she hadn't. The door that led out to the stairway was closed, but unlocked.

No question now. She had gone out.

I had no idea where, and the thought of it gave me a chill. I got dressed and went downstairs and beat on the book store, pressed my face against the windows, but there was no light or movement. I went around to the rear of the building to beat on the back door, to try and wake Martha up in her living quarters, but when I got there I didn't bother. I saw that Martha's van was gone from the carport and Jasmine's car was still in place.

I went back to my apartment and found Jasmine's car keys on the dresser and thought about calling the police, then thought better of it. Their memory of my body-in-the-trunk stunt was a long one, and they might delay. Blow off the whole thing, in fact, mark it up to another aggravation from the boy who cried wolf. If I called Sam it wouldn't be any better. Twice in one night he'd be more likely to kill me than to help me. He was more worried about his pecker than a would-be killer, and he might not do anything at all.

Then I reminded myself it was a game of "What If" and that there wasn't anything to do, nothing to fear. I told myself the worst that could happen would be that Jasmine and Martha would annoy Waldo and make fools of themselves, and then it would all be over for good.

But those thoughts didn't help much, no matter how hard I tried to be convinced. I realized then that it hadn't been just the rain and the humidity that had awakened me. I had been thinking about what Martha said. About Waldo picking a victim later on if we didn't stop him. About the mannequins being a sort of warm-up for what he really wanted to do and would do.

It wasn't just a game anymore. Though I had no real

evidence for it, I believed then what Jasmine and Martha believed.

Waldo the Great was a murderer.

I drove Jasmine's car out to the trailer park and pulled around where we had parked before, and sure enough, there was Martha's van. I pulled in behind it and parked.

I got out, mad as hell, went over to the van and pulled the driver's door open. There wasn't anyone inside. I turned then and looked through the bushes toward the trailer park. Lightning moved to the west and flicked and flared as if it were fireworks on a vibrating string. It lit up the trailer park, made what was obvious momentarily bright and harsh.

Waldo's truck and trailer were gone. There was nothing in its spot but tire tracks.

I tore through the bushes, fought back some blackberry vines, and made the long run over to the spot where Waldo's trailer had been.

I walked around in circles like an idiot. I tried to think, tried to figure what had happened.

I made up a possible scenario: Martha and Jasmine had come out here to spy on Waldo, and maybe Waldo, who kept weird hours, had gone out, and Jasmine and Martha had seen their chance and gone in.

Perhaps Waldo turned around and came back suddenly. Realized he'd forgotten his cigarettes, his money, something like that, and he found Jasmine and Martha snooping.

And if he was a murderer, and he found them, and they had discovered incriminating evidence . . .

Then what?

What would he have done with them?

It struck me then.

The dump. To dispose of the bodies.

God, the bodies.

My stomach soured and my knees shook. I raced back

through the tangled growth, back to Jasmine's car. I pulled around the van and made the circle and whipped onto the road in front of the trailer park and headed for the dump at high speed. If a cop saw me, good. Let him chase me, on out to the dump.

Drops of rain had begun to fall as I turned on the road to the dump. Lightning was crisscrossing more rapidly and more heatedly than before. Thunder rumbled.

I killed the lights and eased into the dump, using the lightning flashes as my guide, and there, stretched across the dump road, blocking passage, was Waldo's trailer. The truck the trailer was fastened to was off the road and slightly turned in my direction, ready to leave the dump. I didn't see any movement. The only sounds were from the throbbing thunder and the hissing lightning. Raindrops were falling faster.

I jerked the car into park in front of the trailer and got out and ran over there, then hesitated. I looked around and spotted a hunk of wood lying in some garbage. I yanked it out and ran back to the trailer and jerked open the door. The smell of dogs was thick in the air.

Lightning flashed in the open doorway and through the thin curtains at the windows. I saw Martha lying on the floor, face down, a meat cleaver in the small of her back. I saw that the bookshelves on the wall were filled with Harlequin romances, and below them nailed onto the shelves, were strange hunks of what in the lightning flashes looked like hairy leather.

Darkness.

A beat.

Lightning flashed.

I looked around, didn't see Waldo hiding in the shadows with another meat cleaver.

Darkness again.

I went over to Martha and knelt beside her, touched her

shoulder. She raised her head, tried to jerk around and grab me, but was too weak. "Sonofabitch," she said.

"It's me," I said.

"Plebin," she said. "Waldo . . . nailed me a few times . . . Thinks I'm dead . . . He's got Jasmine. Tried to stop him . . . Couldn't . . . You got to. They're out . . . there."

I took hold of the cleaver and jerked it out of her back and tossed it on the floor.

"Goddamn," Martha said, and almost did a pushup, but lay back down. "Could have gone all day without that . . . Jasmine. The nut's got her. Go on!"

Martha closed her eyes and lay still. I touched her neck. Still a pulse. But I couldn't do anything now. I had to find Jasmine. Had to hope the bastard hadn't done his work.

I went out of the trailer, around to the other side, looked out over the dump. The light wasn't good, but it was good enough that I could see them immediately. Jasmine, her back to me, upside down, nude, was tied to the inside of the nearest derrick, hung up like a goat for the slaughter. Waldo stood at an angle, facing her, holding something in his hand.

Lightning strobed, thunder rumbled. The poodles were running about, barking and leaping. Two of the dogs were fucking out next to the derrick, flopping tongues. The great black hammer head of the oil pump rose up and went down. Fires glowed from beneath debris and reflected on the metal bars of the derrick and the well pump, and when the rain hit the fires beneath the garbage they gave up white smoke and the smoke rolled in the wind like great balls of cotton, tumbled over Jasmine and Waldo and away.

Waldo swung what he had in his hand at Jasmine. Caught her across the neck with it. Her body twitched. I let out a yell that was absorbed by a sudden peal of thunder and a slash of lightning.

I started running, yelling as I went.

Waldo slashed at Jasmine again, and then he heard me yelling. He stepped to the side and stared at me, surprised. I ran up the little rise that led to the derrick before he could get it together, and as I ducked under a bar on the derrick, he dropped what he was holding.

A long paint brush.

It fell next to a can of dark paint. Rain plopped in the paint and black balls of paint flew up in response and fell down again. One of the dogs jumped the can of paint for no reason I could determine and ran off into the rain.

Jasmine made a noise like a smothered cough. Out of the corner of my eye I could see a strip of thick grey tape across her mouth, and where Waldo had slashed her neck with the brush was a band of paint, dissolving in the rain, running down her neck, over her cheeks and into her eyes and finally her hair, like blood in a black and white movie.

Waldo reached behind his back and came back with a knife. The edge of the blade caught a flash of lightning and gave a wicked wink. Waldo's face was full of expression this time, as if he had saved all his passion for this moment.

"Come on, asshole," I said. "Come on. Cut me."

He leapt forward, very fast. The knife went out and caught me across the chest as I jumped back and hit my head on a metal runner of the derrick. I felt something warm on my chest. Shit. I hadn't really wanted him to cut me. He was a fast little bastard.

I didn't invite him to do that again.

I cocked my piece of wood and let him get as close as I could allow without fear taking over, then I ducked under the metal runner and he ducked under it after me, poking straight out with the knife.

I swung at him, and the wood, rotten, possibly termite ridden, came apart close to my hand and went sailing and crumbling across the dump.

Waldo and I watched the chunk of wood until it hit the dirt by the derrick and exploded into a half dozen fragments.

Waldo turned his attention to me again, smiled, and came fast. I jumped backwards and my feet went out from under me and dogs yelped.

The lover mutts. I had backed over them while they were screwing. I looked up between my knees and saw the dogs turned butt to butt, hung up, and then I looked higher, and there was Waldo and his knife. I rolled and came up and grabbed a wet cardboard box of something and threw it. It struck Waldo in the chest and what was in the box flew out and spun along the wet ground. It was half a mannequin torso.

"You're ruining everything," Waldo said.

I glanced down and saw one of the mannequin legs Sam had pulled from a box and tossed. I grabbed the leg and cocked it on my shoulder like a baseball bat.

"Come on, asshole," I said. "Come on. Let's see if I can put one over the fence with you."

He went nuts then, dove for me. The knife jabbed out, fast and blurry.

I swatted. My swing hit his arm and his knife hand went wide and opened up and the knife flew into a pile of garbage and out of sight.

Waldo and I both looked at where it had disappeared.

We looked at one another. It was my turn to smile.

He staggered back and I followed, rotating the leg, trying to pick up my shot.

He darted to his right, dipped, came up clutching one of the mannequin's arms. He held it by the wrist and smiled. He rotated it the way I had the bat.

We came together, leg and arm swinging. He swung at my head. I blocked with the leg and swung at his knees. He jumped the swing, kicked beautifully while airborne, hit me in the chin and knocked my head back, but I didn't go down.

Four of the poodles came out of nowhere, bouncing and barking beside us, and one of them got hold of my pants leg and started tugging. I hit at him. He yelped. Waldo hit me with the arm across the shoulder. I hit him back with the leg and kicked out and shook the poodle free.

Waldo laughed.

Another of the poodles got hold of his pants legs.

Waldo quit laughing. "Not me, you dumb ingrate!"

Waldo whacked the poodle hard with the arm. It let go, ran off a distance, whirled, took a defiant stance and barked.

I hit Waldo then. It was a good shot, clean and clear and sweet with the sound of the wind, but he got his shoulder up and blocked the blow and he only lost a bit of shirt sleeve, which popped open like a flower blossoming.

"Man, I just bought this shirt," he said.

I swung high to his head and let my body go completely around with the swing, twisting on the balls of my feet, and as I came back around, I lowered the blow and hit him in the ribs. He bellowed and tripped over something, went down and dropped his mannequin arm. Three poodles leapt on his chest and one grabbed his ankle. Behind him, the other two were still hung up, tongues dangling happily. They were waiting for the seasons to change. The next ice age. It didn't matter. They were in no hurry.

I went after Waldo, closing for the kill. He wiped the poodles off his chest with a sweep of his arm and grabbed the mannequin arm beside him, took it by the thick end and stuck it at me as I was about to lower the boom on him. The tips of the mannequin's fingers caught me in the family jewels and a moment later a pain went through me that wasn't quite as bad as being hit by a truck. But it didn't keep me from whacking him over the head with everything I had. The mannequin leg fragmented in my hands and Waldo screamed and rolled and came up and charged me, his forehead streaked with blood, a poodle dangling from one pants leg by the teeth. The poodle stayed with him as he leaped and grabbed my legs at the knees and drove his head into my abdomen and knocked me back into a heap of smoking garbage. The smoke rose up around us and closed over us like a pod and with it came a stink that brought bile to my throat and I felt heat on my back and something sharp like glass and I yelled and rolled with Waldo and the growling poodle and out of the corner of my eye, in mid-roll, I saw another of the poodles had caught on fire in the garbage and was running about like a low-flying comet. We tumbled over some more junk, and over again. Next thing I knew Waldo had rolled away and was up and over me, had hold of six feet of two-by-four with a couple of nails hanging out of the end.

"Goodnight," Waldo said.

The board came around and the tips of the nails caught some light from the garbage fires, made them shine like animal eyes in the dark. The same light made Waldo look like the devil. Then the side of my neck exploded. The pain and shock were like things that had burrowed inside me to live. They owned me. I lay where I was, unable to move, the board hung up in my neck. Waldo tugged, but the board wouldn't come free. He put a foot on my chest and worked the board back and forth. The nails in my neck made a noise like someone trying to whistle through gapped teeth. I tried to lift a hand and grab at the board, but I was too weak. My hands fluttered at my sides as if I were petting the ground. My head wobbled back and forth with Waldo's efforts. I could see him through a blur. His teeth were clenched and spittle was foaming across his lips.

I found my eyes drifting to the top of the oil derrick, perhaps in search of a heavenly choir. Lightning flashed rose-red and sweat-stain yellow in the distance. My eyes fell back to Waldo. I watched him work. My body started trembling as if electrically charged.

Eventually Waldo worked the nails out of my neck. He stood back and took a breath. Getting that board loose was hard work. I noted in an absent kind of way that the poodle had finally let go of his ankle and had wandered off. I felt blood gushing out of my neck, maybe as much as the oil well was pumping. I thought sadly of what was going to happen to Jasmine.

My eyelids were heavy and I could hardly keep them open. A poodle came up and sniffed my face. Waldo finally got his breath. He straddled me and cocked the board and positioned his features for the strike; his face showed plenty of expression now. I wanted to kick up between his legs and hit him in the balls, but I might as well have wanted to be in Las Vegas.

"You're dog food," Waldo said, and just before he swung, my eyes started going out of focus like a movie camera on the fade, but I caught fuzzy movement behind him and there was a silver snake leaping through the air and the snake bit Waldo in the side of the head and he went away from me as if jerked aside by ropes.

My eyes focused again, slowly, and there was Martha, wobbling, holding the golf club properly, end of the swing position. She might have been posing for a photo. The striking end of the club was framed beautifully against the dark sky. I hadn't realized just how pretty her mustache was, all beaded up there in the firelight and the occasional bright throb of the storm.

Martha lowered the club and leaned on it. All of us were pretty tuckered out tonight.

Martha looked at Waldo, who lay face down in the trash, not moving, his hand slowly letting loose of the two-by-four, like a dying octopus relaxing its grip on a sunken ship timber.

"Fore, motherfucker," she said, then she slid down the golf club to her knees. Blood ran out from beneath her wool cap. Things went fuzzy for me again. I closed my eyes as a red glow bloomed to my left, where Waldo's trailer was. It began to rain harder. A poodle licked my bleeding neck.

When I awoke in the hospital I felt very stiff, and I could feel that my shoulders were slightly burned. No flesh missing back there, though, just a feeling akin to mild sunburn. I weakly raised an arm to the bandage on my neck and put it down again. That nearly wore me out.

Jasmine and Martha and Sam came in shortly thereafter. Martha was on crutches and minus her wool cap. Her head was bandaged. Her mustache was clean and well groomed, as if with a toothbrush.

"How's the boy?" Sam said.

"You'd listened, could have been a lot better." I said.

"Yeah, well, the boy that cried wolf and all that," Sam said.

"Jasmine, baby," I said, "how are you?"

"I'm all right. No traumatic scars. Martha got us both out of there."

"I had to rest awhile," Martha said, "but all's well that ends well. You did nearly bleed to death."

"What about you?" I said. "You look pretty good after all that."

"Hey," Martha said, "I've got enough fat and muscle on me to take a few meat cleaver blows. He'd have done better to drive a truck over me. When he caught us sneaking around his trailer, he came up behind me and clubbed me in the head with a meat cleaver before I knew he was there, or I'd have kicked his ass into next Tuesday. After he hit me in the head he worked on me some more when I went down. He should have stuck to my head instead of pounding me in the back. That just tired me out for a while."

"Daddy, there were all kinds of horrid things in his

trailer. Photographs, and . . . there were some pieces of women.''

''Pussies,'' Martha said. ''He'd tanned them. Had one on a belt. I figure he put on and wore it now and then. One of those pervert types.''

''What about old Waldo?'' I asked.

''I made a hole in one on that sonofabitch,'' Martha said, ''but looks like he'll recover. And though the trailer burned down, enough evidence survived to hang him. If we're lucky they'll give his ass the hot needle. Right, Sam?''

''That's right,'' Sam said.

''Whoa,'' I said. ''How'd the trailer burn down?''

''One of the poodles caught on fire in the garbage,'' Jasmine said. ''Poor thing. It ran back to the trailer and the door was open and it ran inside and jumped up in the bed, burned that end of the trailer up.''

''Ruined a bunch of Harlequin Romances,'' Martha said. ''Wish the little fuck had traded those in too. Might have made us a few dollars. Thing is, most of the photographs and the leather pussies survived, so we got the little shit by the balls.''

I looked at Jasmine and smiled.

She smiled back, reached out and patted my shoulder. ''Oh, yeah,'' she said, and opened her purse and took out an envelope. ''This is for you. From Mama.''

''Open it,'' I said.

Jasmine opened it and handed it to me. I took it. It was a get well card that had been sent to Connie at some time by one of her friends. She had blatantly marked out her name, and the sender's name, had written under the canned sentiment printed there, ''Get well, SLOWLY.''

''I'm beginning to think me and your mom aren't going to patch things up,'' I said.

''Afraid not,'' Jasmine said.

''Good reason to move then,'' Martha said. ''I'm getting

out of this one-dog town. I'll level with you. I got a little inheritance I live off of. An uncle left it to me. Said in the will, since I was the ugliest one in the family, I'd need it."

"That's awful," Jasmine said. "Don't you believe that."

"The hell it's awful," Martha said. "I didn't have that money put back to live on, me and those damn books would be on the street. Ugly has its compensations. I've decided to start a book store in LaBorde, and I'm gonna open me a private investigations agency with it. Nice combo, huh? Read a little. Snoop a little. And you two, you want, can be my operatives. You full time, Plebin, and Jasmine, you can work part time while you go to college. What do you think?"

"Do we get a discount on paperbacks?" I asked.

Martha considered that. "I don't think so," she said.

"Air-conditioning?"

"I don't think so."

"Let me consider it," I said.

Suddenly, I couldn't keep my eyes open.

Jasmine gently placed her hand on my arm. "Rest now," she said.

And I did.

STEVEN BRUST

__PHOENIX 0-441-66225-0/$4.50

In the return of Vlad Taltos, sorcerer and assassin, the Demon Goddess comes to his rescue, answering a most heartfelt prayer. How strange she should even give a thought to Vlad, considering he's an *assassin*. But when a patron deity saves your skin, it's always in your best interest to do whatever she wants . . .

__JHEREG 0-441-38554-0/$4.99

There are many ways for a young man with quick wits and a quick sword to advance in the world. Vlad Taltos chose the route of the assassin and the constant companionship of a young jhereg.

__YENDI 0-441-94460-4/$4.99

Vlad Taltos and his jhereg companion learn how the love of a good woman can turn a cold-blooded killer into a <u>real</u> mean S.O.B...

__TECKLA 0-441-79977-9/$4.99

The Teckla were revolting. Vlad Taltos always knew they were lazy, stupid, cowardly peasants...revolting. But now they were revolting against the empire. No joke.

__TALTOS 0-441-18200/$4.99

Journey to the land of the dead. All expenses paid! Not Vlad Taltos' idea of an ideal vacation, but this was work. After all, even an assassin has to earn a living.

__COWBOY FENG'S SPACE BAR AND GRILLE
0-441-11816-X/$3.95

Cowboy Feng's is a great place to visit, but it tends to move around a bit— from Earth to the Moon to Mars to another solar system—And always just one step ahead of whatever mysterious conspiracy is reducing whole worlds to radioactive ash.

"Varley is the best writer in America.
This book proves it." —Tom Clancy

STEEL
BEACH
John Varley

"One of the best science fiction novels of the year...
Nebula and Hugo award-winner Varley makes a
triumphant return!" —*Publishers Weekly*

"Varley's first novel in almost a decade...skillful
science fiction epic...beautifully told." —*Omni*

Fleeing earth after an alien invasion, the human beings
stand on the threshold of evolution, like a fish cast on
artificial shores. Their new home is Luna, a moon colony
blessed with creature comforts, prolonged lifespans, digi-
tal memories, and instant sex-changes. But the people of
Luna are bored, restless, suicidal— and so is the com-
puter that monitors their existence...

An Ace paperback

Coming in August

ALLEN STEELE